Praise for Bonnie Dee's *Evolving Man*

"A boisterous, cheerful romp. Whether you're in the mood for a heart-warming story of redemption or a fun, escapist beach-read, Bonnie Dee always delivers a fantastic romance."

~ *Summer Devon*

"A smart, fun story with timeless romance and ageless sizzle."

~ *Jaci Burton*

Rating: 5 lips "From beginning to end, Bonnie Dee provides non-stop action and sexy, erotic interludes for her readers. I strongly recommend reading Evolving Man because it's unique, sexy, well-written and highly entertaining."

~ *Kerin, Two Lips Reviews*

Evolving Man

Bonnie Dee

A SAMHAIN PUBLISHING, LTD. publication.

Samhain Publishing, Ltd.
512 Forest Lake Drive
Warner Robins, GA 31093
www.samhainpublishing.com

Evolving Man
Copyright © 2007 by Bonnie Dee
Print ISBN: 1-59998-828-7
Digital ISBN: 1-59998-441-5

Editing by Linda Ingmanson
Cover by Vanessa Hawthorne

First Samhain Publishing, Ltd. electronic publication: April 2007
First Samhain Publishing, Ltd. print publication: February 2008

Dedication

To all my loyal readers who follow me from genre to genre since I have the attention span of a gnat and can't stick to one type of story. I appreciate your support of my work and the kind words by email or blog.

Chapter One

"This is a joke, right?" Chrissy ran her hand over the frame of the phone booth-sized cubicle before turning to face her housemate, Lila, lab technician by profession, inventor by calling.

"Absolutely not. With this invention, I'll be able to assemble a group of the greatest, most innovative thinkers of all time. People like Da Vinci, Einstein, Eleanor Roosevelt, Martin Luther King and even great minds from the future. All times are available." Lila's brown eyes glowed with the fervor of a true believer. "A think tank like that could come up with ideas that would change the world!"

"Huh." Sitting in a small chair inside the booth, Taylor, their other housemate, touched the glass surface of the monitor. "Any time, past or future?" There wasn't a trace of skepticism in her voice. She looked up from the monitor, blue eyes wide.

Chrissy didn't know if she admired Taylor's faith in Lila's scientific abilities or despised her naiveté in believing whatever she was told. Despite Taylor's brassy manner, there was a childlike trust about her that Chrissy had lost long ago.

"How does it operate?" Chrissy postponed the inevitable moment when she'd have to admit to Lila she didn't believe in her crazy invention. Over the past few months, the would-be inventor had spent increasing amounts of time in her third-floor lair, which served as both her bedroom and workshop. She'd clearly become mentally unbalanced and somehow both her housemates had completely overlooked it.

Lila drew a deep breath and her voice slowed as though explaining to schoolchildren. "All right, think of it like this: as with radio or television, the invisible waves of time can be captured and viewed here." She tapped the monitor screen, which glowed a ghostly blue. "Simply creating a device to view events in the past or future is remarkable in itself."

To demonstrate, she typed in some information on her keyboard and clicked the mouse. Suddenly a clear image of a stone-pebbled beach on a foggy morning appeared on the monitor. A ship approached the land, slicing through the gray-blue water. It bore the square sails and dragon prow of the Viking ships in 1950s B-movies.

Chrissy leaned against the frame of the booth and watched the show play out. Her worry over Lila's mental health increased. Whatever image was on the monitor, there was no way it could be the real past. More likely Lila had somehow tapped into a satellite signal and was picking up some History Channel broadcast.

"I've taken it a step further than simply viewing moments in time. Not only can my machine show images in time, but it can literally 'capture' a frame and materialize a figure contained in it in the flesh. Right here in this booth."

"Oh, I get it. Like in *Star Trek*. 'Beam me up, Scotty'." Taylor laughed. "It's amazing, Lila."

"Yes, just like *Star Trek*." Lila's voice dripped sarcasm.

On the screen, the marauding Vikings anchored ship and rowed small skiffs toward land. Lila fast-forwarded with a click of the mouse, making the boats race across the water. She slowed the scene again, and the men climbed out of the boats to splash through the shallows toward the beach.

The sailors were tall and muscular, dressed in hide shirts and leggings, their faces almost hidden behind full beards and moustaches. Long, blond hair flowed from beneath their helmets. The Norse warriors brandished swords, pikes and other assorted pointy things as they charged onto the pebbled shore.

Waiting to meet the assault was a much smaller group of men, dressed in fur and leather hides. Remembering a little history, Chrissy guessed they were northern European or Briton villagers facing the marauders. The obvious leader of the defending army was taller and bulkier than his men. His shoulders and chest strained his deer-hide jerkin. Black hair was caught back in a leather thong at the nape of his neck. White teeth flashed against tan skin as he shouted encouragement to the other men, most of whom seemed on the verge of breaking and running before the attacking Vikings. The leader held his sword high and urged his men forward.

Although the moving picture was silent, Chrissy could imagine the man's cries to defend the village and the women and children. She felt sorry for the young leader, in charge of a timid group of fishermen with lame-looking weapons, facing a pack of huge, fierce Norsemen.

The two sides clashed. The fishing folk were definitely outmatched by the invaders. Chrissy cringed as limbs flew and blood spurted.

"Nasty," Taylor murmured. "But, man, that guy's kind of hot." She pointed to one of the Norsemen with flowing gold locks and bared teeth.

Lila frowned and froze the scene. "Typical, Taylor, I'm talking about assembling a think tank to solve the world's problems and you're ogling the men."

"No harm in looking." She shrugged, tossing back her curly, blonde hair.

Chrissy stared at the frozen image of the battle. It was crystal clear down to the details of sunlight glinting off the sharp edges of weapons and blood welling from an open wound. Despite her disbelief, she was intrigued at the prospect of a time-traveling think tank. "How would you communicate with them? Da Vinci didn't speak English, and I'm sure if you talked to one of these guys," she nodded at the screen, "you'd get some incomprehensible dead language."

"Ah." Lila went to her worktable and came back with an earpiece much like a hearing aid. "I've also invented this translating device. It works by reading thought patterns and deciphering them into words the listener understands, rather than translating one language into another. Cool, huh?" Lila beamed, pleased with her own cleverness.

Chrissy stared, feeling terribly guilty she hadn't even noticed her friend was cracking up. Lila spent days holed up here alone on the third floor of the house in her attic workshop. Her friends had always thought of her as an innovative genius with her many ongoing experiments and inventions, but clearly her train had derailed.

Chrissy looked from her insane friend's exultant face to the frozen picture on the screen. The Viking leader and the head defender of the soil were engaged in combat, swords poised ready to thrust. Their mouths were open, shouting. Blood and sweat streaked their bearded faces. The charge of testosterone in the air was almost palpable, and she was embarrassed to feel her crotch tighten simply from staring at the image of the two primitive warriors.

"Well, it's an amazing idea. I can see you've worked hard on it."

"So, exactly how would you do it?" Taylor traced a finger over the Viking seaman's bulging biceps. "I mean, actually pick one and bring him to life?"

"It's like computer animation," Lila explained. "You choose the figure you want to work with, then, instead of manipulating the image as you would in movie making, you press this button and bring him to this moment in time. Your *Star Trek* analogy actually isn't that far off the mark. Basically we're deconstructing molecules and reassembling them here."

"Very cool." Taylor nodded as if it made perfect sense.

Lila did a point and click thing with her mouse and soon the dark-haired barbarian was outlined in red. "See? I've 'cut him out of the picture', so to speak. He's the target now."

Chrissy decided it was time to break the spell. The only way she was going to reach Lila's addled brain was to demonstrate that the machine didn't work. "Then you'd press *this* button?" She reached out and pushed a black button on the left side of the control panel.

"No! Chrissy, don't!" Lila yelled, grabbing at her wrist.

There was a high-pitched, whining sound and the air shimmered then became as opaque as a dark cloud. Chrissy actually felt a change in the density of space around them, a thickening that made the air almost palpable. Suddenly an extra body crowded into the booth with the three women. Chrissy was pressed up against solid muscle, hot, sweaty skin and rank, half-cured animal hides.

The big, bearded man was still roaring his battle cry. Momentum brought his arm down with a mighty slice of his sword, right past Taylor's face. The sword cleaved the monitor screen in two, sending jagged glass shards and electric sparks flying.

All of the women screamed and scrambled to get away. The barbarian bellowed and drew his sword out of the wreckage of the monitor.

As she stumbled from the booth, fighting to keep her balance and run away at the same time, Chrissy caught a glimpse of the man's eyes.

They were wide and confused and they zeroed in on her. He lunged and grabbed her wrist, holding her fast in his powerful grip while yelling something in a language that sounded like pebbles being ground in a cement mixer.

Chrissy screamed at the top of her lungs, a piercing, fire engine wail.

The man dropped her wrist immediately.

She fled across the room.

The barbarian raised his sword, knocking the control panel and sending it crashing onto the floor. He backed out of the booth, holding the sword up in front of him and turning in a slow circle, assessing the room around him.

Shrieking, Taylor ran out the door and clattered down the stairs.

Lila froze near the open door, holding her hands up in a surrendering posture.

Chrissy sidled over to stand shoulder to shoulder with her. It was imperative they didn't let this guy out of the room. She pictured the barbarian hacking his way through the city, maiming pedestrians and stabbing shopkeepers, probably getting run over by a car or shot by the police. They must contain and calm him then send him back where he came from.

The man looked around the room, his gaze darting from one foreign object to another with the panicked air of a wild animal caught in a trap. Finally his attention settled on the two frightened women. Scanning them from head to toe, he spoke again in his guttural language. He took a step toward them, but his manner wasn't threatening, even though he held a big-ass sword in his hands.

"Lila, give him one of those translator thingies," Chrissy muttered. "We have to communicate with him." She smiled broadly at the bearded giant and lifted her open palms to demonstrate her harmlessness.

"Oh... Yeah." Lila startled from her frozen stare. She lifted the ear-piece still clutched in her hand and showed it to the warrior. She carefully hooked it over her ear then held her hands up again.

The man glared at her with those dark brown eyes and said, "Nargatz nia progpadya."

Lila's eyes widened. "Oh, God, no, we're not witches." She took a step toward her work station.

The barbarian feinted right as though to cut her off.

"It's okay. Trust me." She took one slow step after another, hands upraised.

Eyes narrowed, he watched her retrieve a second translator from the bench and hold it out to him.

Chrissy realized she'd been holding her breath when black spots began to dance in front of her eyes. She released the air from her lungs with a whoosh.

The warrior took the device and copied Lila, placing it in his ear.

"Give me one," Chrissy hissed. "I want to know what's going on."

Lila handed her a third translator.

When Chrissy put in the earpiece, the man's garbled words instantly crystallized into coherent thought. It wasn't that she suddenly heard English. It was more like his words engendered images and meaning in her mind.

His fear and dismay translated as, "What's going on here? Who are you? Where am I? Keep away from me or I'll cleave you in two, witches!"

"Not witches." The two women said simultaneously.

"If you'll calm down, I'll try to explain," Lila began.

"Put down the sword then we'll talk," Chrissy commanded.

"I invented a machine and it brought you into the future." Lila indicated the booth in the center of the room.

"Set it down slowly. There's nobody here who's going to hurt you." Chrissy gazed at him with what she hoped was a soothing expression.

The bearded man looked back and forth between the two women then slowly lowered the point of his sword to the floor. "What have you done to me?"

"It was an accident. I didn't believe Lila's machine worked and I pressed a button."

"Machine?" He frowned and Chrissy caught the images the word meant to him—a hand cart and a simple pulley to draw water up from the village well.

"It's not magic," Lila said. "There are scientific principles involved."

"She'll try to return you to where you came from, but it might take a while, since you broke the machine with your sword."

The warrior glanced at the broken monitor then back at the women, examining their clothing, their faces and the room again. "Where is this place?"

Chrissy explained as simply as she could. "We are in a land far from yours and in a different time many years in the future. Do you understand?"

"Why?" He glared at her, his grip on the sword not relaxing.

"Because Lila thought it would be a good thing to talk to people from other times. She thought we could learn useful things from them." Chrissy smiled as though at an embarrassing faux pas. "We didn't mean to bring *you* here."

He raised an eyebrow and stared at her with piercing eyes. "You think you have nothing to learn from me?"

"No. I mean, yes. Of course, you're a great warrior and have important skills, very...admirable skills, but they aren't something we can use in our society." She gestured at the ruins of the time machine. "This is an experiment

16

gone wrong. We certainly didn't mean to drag you out of your life and into ours." The adrenaline surging through her system was having the odd effect of making her nipples tingle and her crotch ache. That was the only explanation for her body's reaction to the barbarian's dark, glittering gaze.

He continued to regard her, but his white-knuckled grip on the sword hilt loosened.

Chrissy turned to Lila. "We should stop Taylor before she calls 911 and we have to explain this guy to the police."

"Yeah." Lila started for the door.

The warrior raised his weapon again.

"It's all right," Lila said. "I'm just going to get our friend, the other woman you saw."

"Where are your men?" He turned his attention back to Chrissy after Lila left. "You women live alone?"

A warm flush suffused her as his intense gaze roved over her body. "Well, the three of us share this house, yes. We want to stop our friend before she calls the police—the, uh, guardians of our village. They wouldn't understand your presence here and there might be trouble."

"Three women living together? You must be witches then...or whores, I would guess from your clothing." The way his eyes scanned every inch of her flesh not covered by her tank top or shorts made her stomach flip.

"No! Neither one. In our time women often live on their own and have jobs, and all the girls dress like this."

Chrissy realized she'd used the same words in middle school arguing with her mother about her wardrobe. She felt her cheeks burn and wished she were at least wearing jeans.

After a last, lingering look at her legs, the man announced, "You are very thin. Women in my village have stronger legs and bigger hips, good for working in the field and bearing children."

"Huh, imagine that." Chrissy searched for something to say. "You're, um…taller than I would have expected." Everything she'd seen on the History Channel had led her to believe a man from an earlier century would be short. This guy was over six feet tall. Maybe he was some kind of giant among his people.

She tried to picture him without the beard and moustache. His sculpted cheekbones gave her the impression he might be quite good looking under all the wild hair. Attractive even, if you could get past the stench. Now that things had calmed down, she was excruciatingly aware of the powerful smell of old sweat and dirty animal hides. Any notions she'd ever entertained about a barbarian lover like those in romance novels evaporated.

Nervously, she tapped her fingers against the sides of her legs and cleared her throat. "Until my friend can fix the machine and get you back home, we'll show you the modern world. Things have changed completely since your day." She thought about men beating the crap out of each other in fights or killing each other on battlefields. "Well, maybe not so much. People are still pretty violent."

Lila reappeared in the doorway with Taylor by her side. For a moment, Chrissy saw them through the stranger's eyes: statuesque, dark-skinned, black-haired Lila and short, busty, blonde Taylor, a perfect contrasting pair. Then she imagined what she might look like to him: medium height, medium build, medium red-brown hair. She was nothing special.

Lila stepped into the room. "Sir, I want to apologize for taking you from your world. I'll get right to work fixing the machine so I can put you back where you came from."

Taylor's eyes were huge as she gaped at the tall, broad-shouldered, battle-scarred barbarian in their midst, but she followed Lila into the room.

"What's your name?" Chrissy asked.

He growled something that sounded like 'G'rath' but her translator reconfigured it into Gareth.

She smiled and inclined her head. "Pleased to meet you, Gareth. I'm Chrissy. This is Lila and Taylor."

Lila muttered to herself as she walked past their time traveler to squat by her destroyed invention. Already she'd tuned them all out and entered her zone of calculations and equations.

Gareth turned as she passed so all three women were still in his sight. He continued to heft his sword and watch them warily. "Would you like something to eat?" Taylor asked, overcoming her awestruck silence and resuming her natural chattiness. "I could make you a sandwich or an omelet. What do you like to eat? Probably a lot of wild game, huh? Well, I don't really cook meat. I'm

19

a vegetarian, myself. But the way I fix an enchilada you can't even tell it's stuffed with veggies and tofu. I cut the vegetables up really fine and marinate them in my own special sauce for a few hours before I stir-fry them. Then I take—"

"Taylor, go cook." Chrissy turned back to their guest with her fake smile etched on her face. "Maybe you'd like to clean up before you eat? I'll show you how modern plumbing works. I think you'll be interested in this." He seemed reluctant to follow her from the room. The upper part of his face was pale against the dark hair of his moustache and beard. Streaks of blood and dirt marked his forehead and cheeks. He swayed a little and Chrissy feared he might pass out. She could appreciate his wooziness, torn from the adrenaline rush of battle to face a bizarre new world. She'd have been hysterical or hyperventilating if she was him.

She walked over to him and put a hand on his arm. Looking up into his worried, deep brown eyes, for the first time she offered a genuine smile. "Come with me. It'll be all right."

The world around Gareth spun. The air was thick and choking. Distant, unidentifiable sounds from outside the room bombarded his hearing. He'd only felt this close to fainting one other time, after fasting for two days before his manhood ceremony. During the long rites, he'd been disoriented and light-headed. Only his father's proud gaze had kept him from succumbing to darkness and tumbling to the ground. Gareth would not humiliate himself or his family in front of the village, so he stayed upright by willpower alone.

Now he stared down into the woman's, Chrissy's, eyes and felt her small hand on his forearm. Once more he used willpower to steady his backbone and clear his head. It was inconceivable to show weakness in front of the witches. Until he figured out what evil scheme they were up to, he must keep his wits about him.

And, they must never guess he was afraid.

The women's appearance and manners were strange. The one touching his arm had brown hair with a deep red cast to it and the smoothest, palest skin he'd ever seen. With her shoulder-length hair he might have taken her for a boy but for the evidence of her womanliness beneath the small top she wore. Her breasts jutted against soft fabric the color of lilacs. She wore short pants on her lower half and her naked legs were on display. Gareth could hardly pull his gaze away from her shapely calves and thighs.

The woman named Lila was even more amazing. Her skin was browner than a hazelnut all over, not tanned by the sun, but naturally dark. Her black hair was cut even shorter than Chrissy's and fluffed around her face in tight curls. Her features were exotic, a wide nose and full magenta lips.

The one they called Taylor had hair as yellow as that of the invaders from the north. He wondered if she was of their tribe. She yammered more words in their incomprehensible language—perhaps casting a spell on

21

him—then, with a wave of her hand, turned and left the room.

After examining the witches and the indecipherable objects cluttering the room, all made from foreign materials, Gareth was convinced he had indeed been taken to a different place and time. Either that or he was dead and this was what was really on the other side of the grave.

The woman called Chrissy took his arm, leading him from the room and down a flight of stairs—not crooked and warped like the ladder steps in the larger houses of his village, but perfectly spaced and absolutely even.

She guided him down a short hallway to a room containing two basins made of white stone. One was shaped like a stool and was half full of water. Perhaps it was an indoor well. He was suddenly so thirsty he wanted to fall to his knees beside it and scoop handfuls of water to his mouth. The other basin was smaller, about waist high and empty. Across one end of the room was a curtain cunningly woven of shiny thread and dyed with images of colorful fishes swimming in water.

Gareth stared awestruck at the amazing cloth mural. Even the chapel back home had no artwork to compare with these exquisite fishes. He looked with new respect at Chrissy. Witch or whore, she was obviously a woman of wealth in her world to possess such a marvelous painting.

"This is a sink," Chrissy said, pointing to the small basin. "These handles turn the water on and off. This one's hot and this one's cold. The water comes out here at the faucet." She demonstrated. "We use this room for cleaning up."

She told him the other basin was called a toilet and showed him how it flushed away bodily waste, then she gave him soap and cloths for washing and drying his body. Pulling back the fish curtain, she revealed a deep basin on the floor.

"This is a tub. You're going to take a shower to get clean. See?" Chrissy turned a knob and made an instant waterfall.

Gareth stepped back, startled by the gushing flow. He would have been even more fascinated by the magic if the woman wasn't half-naked and standing so close to him. Her body was very distracting. He'd never seen hair so shiny and bright nor skin so smooth and unblemished. He longed to reach out and touch Chrissy, to feel the reality of her flesh. The brief moment he'd held her wrist in his hand upon his arrival in this place it had seemed real enough, warm and pulsing against his palm. Her bones were tiny and delicate like the leg of a fawn. When she'd screamed, he'd let go instantly, afraid he'd hurt her.

"Okay?" Chrissy asked.

Gareth's attention jerked back to the present.

"Do you understand what you're supposed to do? Shampoo, soap, deodorant?"

"Yes."

"Leave your clothes on the floor. I'll bring you fresh things to wear so you'll blend in better, okay?"

"Yes."

After she closed the door and left, it occurred to him that she and her coven might be gathering warriors to imprison or kill him. When her sweet, honeyed voice poured over him, it was too easy to forget his intention to remain on guard. It was obviously witchcraft lulling him into complacency. He decided not to wash in the water lest it cast a spell of oblivion or weakness over him. Instead he sat on the floor by the white stool, laid his sword carefully on the ground and rested his aching head on his knees, wrapping his arms around them.

"Lila, are you going to be able to fix this?" Chrissy heard her voice rising on the edge of panic, but was helpless to control the shrillness.

"I don't know! And yelling isn't helping me concentrate." Lila poked at the remnants of the monitor and control panel. "I'm going to have to reconstruct almost all of this." She sounded close to tears. "Jesus, why'd you have to press that button?"

Humiliated at her part in the disaster, Chrissy changed the subject. "Look, I've got to go to the store and buy this guy some clothes to wear. Are you and Taylor going to be okay here? I mean, do you think he's safe? I couldn't get him to give up that sword."

Lila didn't answer. She was already calculating the computer parts she'd need.

Leaving her to her work, Chrissy went down to the second floor. She stopped at the bathroom door to listen for the sound of the shower running, but no noise came from inside. She knocked on the door. "Hey, are you still in there, Gareth?"

A muffled voice said, "Yes."

"Aren't you going to get cleaned up?"

The door opened and Gareth stood in the doorway, fully clothed. "Why is it so important to you? Have you put a spell on the water to rob me of my wits or drain my strength?"

"No!" She was torn between wanting to laugh at his primitive superstitions and feeling a frisson of excited fear at his aggressive posture and narrowed eyes.

"Then let me see *you* enter the waterfall first." Gareth suddenly seized her wrist and manhandled her across the room. He turned on the water as she'd showed him and thrust her into the tub under the spray.

"Yeow!" Chrissy cried as cold water drenched her body. "Turn it off!" Her wet shirt clung to her chest and her nipples pebbled hard against the material. She quickly crossed her arms over her breasts as she stood beneath the streaming water and glared at Gareth. "Satisfied? The water isn't tainted." Shivering, she moved from under the showerhead to the back half of the tub.

Gareth stood before her looking large and dangerous and wild. His grip on her wrist never lessened, making her aware of the power in his big-muscled arms. His gaze was riveted on her wet body and his fears about the shower seemed to have been replaced by an even more elemental concern. A flicker of mingled unease and arousal blossomed in her. He was a primitive man. Would he simply take what he desired? Would she fight him if he did?

Chrissy squared her shoulders and adopted her mother's critical, irritated tone, the one she'd heard so much growing up. "Take your translator off before you go in. It might short out or something." She reached toward Gareth's ear to remove the device and he jerked away. Put off balance by the unexpected move, she slipped on the wet ceramic of the tub and pitched forward.

Gareth caught her, pressing her against his hard chest. She was surrounded in the odor of his hot, male body. Suddenly the ripe smell of sweat seemed more sexy than stinky.

She relaxed in his embrace for a second before pushing against his chest with both hands and straightening. Stepping out of the shower with as much dignity as she could muster, she grabbed a towel and wrapped it around herself. "You can go in now. It's safe," she said acidly.

Her earpiece must have gotten water in it, because the last thing she heard before leaving the bathroom was a growled, "H'nash grottweib un ziesch." Chrissy shut the door and leaned against it, breathing hard, totally humiliated by her body's instant arousal around the stranger. Just because she hadn't been on a date in months was no reason for her to lose her shit over some random barbarian from another century who dropped in unannounced.

She went to her room and changed into fresh clothes—jeans and a long-sleeved shirt this time—then stopped by the kitchen to check in with Taylor before leaving for the store. "Hey, how's it going?"

"Freaky. I can't get over the weirdness." Taylor neatly cracked an egg into a bowl. "How about you?"

"My freak-meter is off the charts. Gareth is showering upstairs and I'm going to go buy something for him to wear. For God's sake, don't let him get back in those buckskins. They reek. Take and hide them somewhere."

"Got it. What's Lila doing?"

"Trying to fix her damn machine." Chrissy shook her head. "I can't believe it actually worked."

"I can't believe you pushed the button."

She drove to the nearest department store and chose the cheapest jeans, shirts, underwear and shoes she could find. Even so, the new wardrobe set her back a couple hundred bucks she couldn't afford.

Returning home less than an hour later, Chrissy walked into the kitchen and stopped short at the sight of the stunning male specimen sitting at the kitchen table wolfing down an omelet. Taylor had cut Gareth's hair and shaved him, leaving just a thin line of beard to enhance his jawline. His face was all sharp angles and planes, prominent cheekbones, a straight nose and strong jaw. Only his lips, framed by a neatly trimmed moustache, were full and soft looking. He wore a blue towel wrapped around his waist and his naked torso was an eye opener.

His body was sinewy and hard with the kind of muscle gained from honest manual labor rather than pumping iron at a gym. Gareth glanced up when Chrissy entered the room and his dark eyes with their ridiculously long lashes made her catch her breath.

A fashion magazine lay open beside his plate. The male models inside sported the latest styles. Taylor stood beside his chair explaining the evolution of men's suits and the current trend toward little or no facial hair. "So, you see, in our culture no one wants the venerable look a full, bushy beard gives. Everyone's trying to look younger, not older. Hairlessness on men's and women's bodies is very 'in' right now. I could wax your chest for you if you want. Oh, hi, Chrissy." Taylor smiled at her. "I'm trying to convince Gareth to go all the way and let me shave the rest of his beard off."

"He's not going to be here long," Chrissy reminded her. "When he returns to his own time, he has to fit in. You can't change up his look too much."

"Schmelfelt dur croynid." Gareth pointed to a picture in the magazine.

Chrissy reached in her purse, located the translator and reinserted it in her ear. Evidently the water hadn't permanently damaged it because his next words came in clearly. "These men look like boys." He flipped the fashion magazine closed. "I am not a child. I will not shave off my beard."

No you're definitely not a child. Chrissy gave his body another admiring once-over. *Not at all.* Out loud she said,

"Looks good as it is, Taylor. Very Russell Crowe in *Gladiator.*"

"Thank you!" Taylor fluffed a hand through Gareth's glossy black curls and Chrissy felt a ridiculous surge of annoyance at the familiar gesture.

"I have some clothes for you if you'd like to try them on." She held her two bags full of purchases toward him.

"Yeah, I took his clothes and put them down in the laundry. I'm not sure how to clean animal hides," Taylor said.

Gareth stood to follow Chrissy from the room. The blue towel slipped on his hips and before he caught and adjusted it, she caught a glimpse of dark pubic hair and the head of his semi-rigid penis.

Swallowing hard, she glanced up to see him noticing her quick appraisal of his assets. A slight smirk curved his lips and that touch of amusement made his saturnine good looks even more arresting. Chrissy abruptly turned and led the way from the kitchen and upstairs. The sound of his bare feet, padding up the steps behind her, set the hair on her arms prickling.

There was no denying the red-haired witch aroused him. Her interested look at his cock had instantly stiffened it, but even before that, Gareth was attracted to Chrissy. From the moment he'd grabbed her fragile wrist and searched her green eyes for an explanation for his jolting arrival into this strange world, he'd felt a strange magnetism drawing him to her. The sight of her wet clothes clinging to her body under the cascading water was permanently etched in his mind.

It had been too long since he'd bedded a wench. That was the problem. He'd been too busy to woo a woman and had remained solitary too long. That was why, despite the bizarre circumstances of the day which should take up every bit of his attention, his body reacted so strongly to hers. Either that or she truly had bewitched him. He wondered what her bright, flame-colored hair would feel like in his hands. Would it be cool and smooth as silk or would it burn?

As he walked up the cleverly constructed steps to the upper level of the dwelling, his gaze fastened on Chrissy's ass in the tight boy's pants she wore. Her firm cheeks swayed hypnotically from side to side and he had an urge to reach out and grab them—grab *her,* sling her over his shoulder and carry her off to bed.

"I hope these clothes fit." Chrissy turned at the top of the stairs to face him.

Gareth's attention snapped from her rear up to her face.

"I guessed on your sizes." She handed him the slippery bags, which appeared to be made from the same strange cloth as the shiny fabric with the fishes. She directed him to the bathing room to dress.

He was entranced by each article of clothing he pulled from the bag. The undergarments, wrapped in a different kind of clear, shiny material, were as white and soft as rose petals against his skin. He slipped the tunic over his head and stepped into the short pants and stockings—held up around his calves without lacing. Gareth wondered what it would take for the women of his village to be able to spin and weave such amazing fabrics.

The long, blue pants were made of a coarse, sturdy material compared to the underclothes, but were still more comfortable than any leggings he'd ever worn. The cream-colored shirt fastened with ingenious small discs up the front, which slipped into tiny slits in the fabric.

Looking at himself in the reflecting glass, Gareth was amazed at the transformation in his appearance. His new short hair made his whole head feel lighter. The edge tickled where it brushed against his neck. His beard and moustache had been trimmed to accentuate his jaw and lips and he had to admit the effect was striking.

He touched the slick surface of the glass, drawing his lips back from his teeth and examining them. He'd never seen his reflection so unwavering and clear. This must be how he looked to other people. The reflective glass was yet another example of the amazing craftsmanship of these future humans.

Gareth walked back out into the hallway to find Chrissy waiting.

From the widening of her eyes, the woman approved his new apparel. "You look great." She gave him a smile that made his pulse speed up. A little crease appeared in her right cheek and he wanted to dip his fingertip in the indentation and feel the warmth of her soft cheek.

"How are you holding up?" she continued. "This must be extremely stressful and overwhelming. Everything you see and hear must be different from anything you've ever experienced before."

Gareth thought, *Except the rush and the longing in my loins every time I look at you, which is exactly how I used to feel whenever I saw Colwen's wife, Marjoli...hungry.* "Yes," he said. "It is difficult to understand this world, but I want to learn more about it."

"I'll show you some books with pictures and maybe I can find a program on TV that will give you a little of the history you've missed."

"No, don't!" The dark-skinned witch was descending the stairs from her magic room. She intercepted them in the hallway and spoke to Chrissy. "You must keep him as isolated as possible. Any information about the future could influence him to change his society and consequently the course of history."

"It's a little late now to be worrying about the space-time continuum, Doc!" Chrissy snapped. "What were you planning to do with your think tank of brainiacs? Kidnapping Socrates, Einstein and Mother Theresa would certainly have altered the world."

Lila frowned. "All right. Maybe I didn't think it through completely, but all my ideas were theoretical until *you* pushed the button! Please, take Gareth and do something quiet and non-interactive with him while I try to fix the damn machine."

Gareth's gaze shot back and forth between the two arguing women. Half of their words broadcast images that were almost indecipherable, beyond his realm of comprehension. It infuriated him. He didn't like feeling like a child among adults, too ignorant to join in the discussion about his own life.

Lila walked toward the bathing room, went in and closed the door behind her.

Chrissy turned to Gareth. "Would you like to lie down and rest? I'm sure with the battle and the time travel you must be exhausted. A nap until dinner is what you need."

She was right. He was stretched to his emotional limit, trying to comprehend the events of the day. His head ached and he wanted to close his eyes to shut out the barrage of foreign sights. He felt dizzy from taking in so much new information. But he didn't like her mothering tone of voice. It belittled his manhood. "I am not tired," Gareth said, aware that he sounded like a sulky child.

"All right, then. I won't show you anything about world history or science or anything that could put ideas into your head, but I'll put in a movie."

The last word was accompanied by bright colors and rapid images. Gareth had no idea what they meant, but he agreed. "Yes, a moo-vee would be good."

Chrissy led him downstairs to yet another room in this huge house. He wondered how three lone women could afford to live in such luxury. She bade him relax on a soft, cushioned piece of furniture called a couch then pressed a button on a square box. Moving images blossomed on the shiny front of the box.

People rode in shiny, covered carts without horses at astonishing speeds down hard, black roads. A naked woman lathered her legs under the pounding water of a shower while loud music played. A man looked directly at Gareth and spoke about thunderstorms. Then the smooth surface of the box went bright blue before being filled by yet more images.

"I think you're really going to like this," Chrissy said, sitting on the other chair in the room. "It should be something you can relate to."

On the screen, a village much like Gareth's filled the screen. A boy dressed in somewhat familiar garb came into view. Gareth stared, entranced at first by the images themselves then focusing on the story that went with the moving pictures. It told the tale of a warrior defending his people. Gareth barely noticed when Taylor came into the room.

"Oh, *Braveheart*. Good choice, Chrissy." She flopped down on a chair.

Gareth relaxed on the long, comfortable couch, watching the movie until his aching eyes drifted closed.

"Look, he's asleep," Taylor said. "How cute! And he's such a hottie."

Chrissy looked from Mel Gibson to the real life warrior, sound asleep on their couch and tried to wrap her mind around the concept that this very live, flesh and blood man was the same person they'd watched on a computer monitor, engaged in a battle to the death only a couple of hours earlier. It was impossible to believe even though they'd experienced it firsthand. She wondered if they'd ever be able to return him to his home. She could comprehend the concept of plucking someone out of the waves of time and bringing him to the present, but didn't know how Lila's machine could deposit him safely back in his own moment in history.

She also couldn't imagine Gareth wanting to give up the luxuries he'd experienced today to return to a freezing hovel with no running water. But there were probably people he cared about in his world, family members, maybe a wife and children. Of course those ties would outweigh the attraction of any creature comforts the twenty-first century could offer.

"You did a great job with the hair and beard," Chrissy told Taylor. "I'm not usually a fan of facial hair, but he looks really good."

"I know. It took some convincing to get him to agree to it, but you know how persuasive I can be."

Chrissy had a sudden mental image of buxom Taylor circling around a seated Gareth, combing out his wet hair and snipping it short. She pictured Taylor moving in close so her breasts were practically in his face as she lathered and shaved his neck and trimmed his moustache and beard. Chrissy felt another stab of irritation. Taylor was such a flirt.

The two women watched the sleeping man's handsome face for a moment.

"Chrissy, you haven't been on a date in, like, a year," Taylor suddenly said. "You're always saying you wish you could meet a man without the hang-ups and mommy issues so many modern guys have. Gareth might be your chance to have no-strings-attached, old-fashioned fun. He's about as manly a man as you could hope to find and he's going back where he came from soon, so why not have a fling while he's here?"

"Because, no! That's crazy. Besides, we're not supposed to interact with Gareth any more than necessary, according to Lila, in case it messes up the future."

"So don't talk, just fuck. I'm sure a little sex couldn't hurt anything."

"'Just fuck'. Sage advice, Taylor."

"Here's a little saying my mama told me, 'When a man is hot, time to take a shot'." She waggled her eyebrows and crossed one leg over the other, jiggling her foot.

There were several beats of silence. "What makes you think he even wants to?" Chrissy asked.

"Please. Have you seen him looking at you? Besides, men *always* want to. Always."

That was true enough, and damn Taylor for planting the seed. Chrissy couldn't stop thinking about it now. Although if she was honest, she had to admit the seed had been planted the moment she'd tumbled into Gareth's arms wet from the shower. It was simply germinating now thanks to Taylor's words.

She took another look at Gareth, arms crossed over his rising and falling chest. The shirt she'd bought him was a little too small and it stretched across his broad shoulders. His lips were parted; quiet breaths whistled through them. Thick, dark lashes fanned across his cheeks. His legs, encased in blue denim, were long, the bulge in the crotch prominent.

Before, when Chrissy had looked at him she'd seen a problem to be solved. Now all she saw was sex. Damn, Taylor!

Gareth dreamed.

He was in the heat of battle, his sword flashing and impaling his foe. Warm blood spattered his face. He felt the firm resistance of flesh as he withdrew his sword from the body before him. The sounds of combat around him faded to a distant roar and all he could hear was his own heartbeat and blood rushing in his ears. All he could see was the tall, blond warrior whom he must slay. The world was simple. It was life or death.

Suddenly the dream changed. *His opponent disappeared, replaced by a woman with hair glowing coppery red. Her eyes were as wide as a doe's, but green as meadow grass. She screamed into his face like a wildcat. Her wrist felt thin and delicate as he pulled her to him, covering her mouth with his, cutting off her scream. Her mouth was hot and tasted like honey.*

Her full breasts were smashed up against his chest and her crotch pressed into his raging hard-on. His arms were full of womanly softness and he had to have her now. He began to tear away her clothes...

Gareth woke with a jerk, sitting up straight and gasping for air. He blinked and looked around the room. On the square picture box a battle was taking place, hundreds of warriors facing off over an open field, many of them with blue-painted faces. He glanced toward Chrissy's chair. She slept. Taylor had left the room.

Gareth rubbed his eyes and yawned. He felt much better for having slept, although dizziness and disorientation suffused him again as he took in the absolute foreignness of the room. And this was only one house. How much more had changed in the world, if this was really the future as the women claimed? What other wonders had mankind wrought? The women intended to keep him isolated until Lila repaired her machine and returned him to his own time, but he wanted to see this new world.

He stood.

Chrissy stirred in her chair, but didn't wake. He resisted the urge to stoop over her and touch her hair or stroke her skin to feel its texture. Instead he walked silently from the room then out the front door of the house.

Inside the house, he'd been aware of odd sounds coming from all around him—the large cooling chest in the kitchen, for example. Its machinery made a continuous low hum. The picture box with the movie also made that humming sound. Whatever force operated these things droned like a bee. Outside the house, the din of strange noises deafened him.

Gareth stood on the step and stared at the amazing sights surrounding him. On the black road in front of him passed many carts without horses like the ones he'd seen on the picture box. Their roars hurt his ears and the smell they left behind choked him.

Walking on paths on either side of the road were people in an unbelievable array of clothing in many colors and styles. The people themselves were as varied as their apparel. Skin shades ranged from ghost pale to deepest black and their hair was blond, brown, black, red and even blue. Gareth gaped at a blue-haired boy gliding past on a flat board with tiny wheels. Glittering rings pierced the boy's eyebrow and lip. He caught Gareth's stare and glared back him, raising his hand and holding up his middle finger.

Gareth descended the steps to the white footpath. He half-expected people to point at him and stare, or run from him in fear, but they passed by without a second look. Wearing these clothes, he looked like them; the people thought he was one of them. No one knew he was a powerful warrior and they didn't see he was a foreigner in their world.

Gareth strolled past two women in light, fluttering dresses and tall shoes. They were deep in conversation, their voices high-pitched and their gestures extravagant.

One of them glanced his way, scanned his body up and down then smiled before moving on.

A man and woman pushing a handcart with a baby in it came toward him. The woman also held a leather strip attached to a dog's collar. She pulled the dog close to her side and told it to behave as they walked past Gareth. Seeing the family group made his chest tighten. He thought of his own relatives and wondered if he'd ever see them again.

Breathing in the acrid-smelling air, he tried to get his bearings, but was overwhelmed by the assault of noise and movement all around him. He looked up at the sky. The cloudy, blue arc was the same, although the glowing disc of the sun appeared hazy. Then a strange bird sailed high overhead leaving a trail of white behind it, and Gareth knew that even the sky had been touched by man. The bird was clearly another machine. He didn't know whether to be impressed or dismayed by the vast changes people had made in the world.

Across the road, there were trees and grass. People walked or sat on benches in the little refuge of nature. Gareth wanted to go there, but the loud carts rumbled in a steady stream between him and the grassy land. Then he noticed a group of people up ahead all crossing the road together while the carts waited for them to pass. He walked over and joined the queue, feeling like a sheep being herded with its flock as he crossed the black road.

The little piece of natural land was bigger than he'd thought. Paths ran through it and in the center a man-made spring of water gushed high into the air then cascaded down into a large, round pool. Children splashed in the water while their mothers chatted nearby. An old woman fed birds from her seat on a bench.

Gareth stopped near two men hunched over a game board and watched them move black and red discs. Then he moved on, found an empty bench and sank down. He continued to watch the passing people, intrigued by the infinite variety of life.

"Chrissy, wake up! He's gone." Taylor's voice swam through thick layers of her consciousness, rousing her from deep sleep.

"What?" She sat up and wiped a hand across her cobwebbed eyes.

"Gone. Flown the coop. I checked every room."

"Shit." Chrissy was on her feet and out the door in less than a minute, with Taylor on her heels. She stood on the front stoop looking up and down the street, her heart pounding. She felt like a mother whose child had wandered off. Which direction would Gareth go when every place was equally foreign to him? "I'll go right. You go left," she directed Taylor.

Chrissy walked two blocks then her brain kicked in as she stared across the street at the park. It was a cool, green haven in the midst of all the concrete. It would look like home to Gareth. Crossing the street, she walked along one of the paths until she found him sitting on a park bench. The strong masculinity of his profile as he watched the children swing on the playground made her stomach flutter. He was exactly the kind of man who most attracted her, big, built like a rock, dark-haired and with deep, expressive eyes that displayed a secret sensitivity under his alpha-maleness.

"Hey." She dropped down on the bench beside him.

Gareth turned to look at her with a glassy-eyed expression that hinted he was beyond overwhelmed and near shutdown mode.

She rested her hand on his arm, rubbing it sympathetically.

His gaze dropped to her hand. "It's all so different here. I can't..." He shook his head, running out of words.

She stroked the back of his hand. "I know. I mean, I can imagine. Look, why don't you come back to the house with me? Lila is working really hard on fixing the machine. I'm sure she'll have you back where you belong by tomorrow and you can pretend this was all a dream."

He took her hand and his grip was so strong Chrissy thought her bones might be crushed.

"Come on." She rose, drawing him to his feet. "It'll be all right. Come with me."

Gareth stood beside her like a small mountain, but continued grasping her hand like a small boy.

Together they walked down the gravel path, holding hands as if they were a couple.

Chapter Two

It was after midnight. Lila rested her head in her hands, massaging her temples and glaring at the broken pieces of her machine. She'd already replaced the monitor. It was just a plain computer screen she'd salvaged from one of her older PCs. The control board was the problem. Gareth had cleaved it in two and it was not a standard computer keyboard. Lila had worked on it for over a year, creating a scientific marvel that could do the impossible.

She patiently sorted through the wreckage of tiny bits and pieces, laying aside what was still salvageable. The task was painstaking and she felt the crunch of time working against her. Not only was her invention in ruins, but a primitive man was stuck in the present. What kind of chaos might that interrupted life cause? She'd never intended to bring people to the present on a permanent basis, only borrow them for a while, interview them, pick their brains then send them back to their own times to resume their place in history.

She needed help, a second brain and someone with a quick mind and nimble fingers who could help her reassemble this mess and be trusted to never tell a soul.

Lila turned to her laptop and logged on to the instant messenger program.

Logorhythmic: Hey, MathMan, are you on?

MathMan: Yeah. What's up?

Logorhythmic: Problem. You know that project I've been working on?

MathMan: The one you'll only hint at? You've got me so curious it's all I can think about.

Logorhythmic: That's the one. I'm in big trouble. Huge!

MathMan: How can I help?

Lila hesitated then typed. Logorhythmic: I think it's time we finally met in person.

There was a pause before MathMan returned: I've been waiting for the day!

Chrissy lay on her pallet of couch cushions on the floor of Taylor's room and stared at the square of streetlight shining against the wall. An occasional car headlight traveled across the same wall. There was creaking on the other side of that wall as Gareth turned over in Chrissy's bed.

Her bed. She pictured his naked torso stretched out beneath her covers, his dark head lying on her pillow, the sheets maybe slipping down his dark-haired chest. Then she pictured herself lying beside him and shivered.

Grunting, she flipped over onto her side. The floor hurt her shoulder through the thin cushion. She plumped her pillow and tried to match her breathing to Taylor's steady, even breaths, hoping it would lull her to sleep. But her mind replayed every moment of the amazing afternoon. She relived the sensation of being held tight against Gareth's big body, breathing in his overpowering scent, feeling the rough animal hide against her cheek. She remembered how strong his arms were when he caught her in the bathroom. Then she pictured him dressed in modern clothes with his hair and beard neatly trimmed, asleep on their couch.

It had been way too long since Chrissy had been with a man. Her last boyfriend, Dave, had destroyed her trust. She'd enjoyed a few brief encounters since Dave, but nothing permanent. Chrissy had come to the conclusion that her vibrator made a suitable substitute for the heartache men inevitably brought, and she could switch if off and put it away when she was done with it.

But tonight, she was itchy and anxious and hungry for the man lying so near and yet so far on the other side of the wall. After half an hour of fruitlessly pursuing sleep, Chrissy got up and walked down the hall to the bathroom. As she passed her bedroom, she slowed, stopped and stared at the closed door for a full minute. She shook her head and walked on, poured a glass of water in the bathroom then started back up the darkened hall.

A shadowy figure stood framed in her bedroom doorway. Her heart pounded in her chest and she almost cried out.

Gareth was naked, his body a pale blur in the dark.

Chrissy strained to see him in the dim light.

He stepped into the hall and she got an eyeful of man.

His shoulders were broad and his biceps bigger in circumference than her thighs. He looked like he could lift a semi single-handedly. His chest was deep and chiseled with a light smattering of dark hair across it and his abdomen was a marvel of angles and planes with a flat stomach that veed down into narrow hips. Gareth's cock thrust out proudly from a dark tangle of pubic hair. Heavy balls swung below it.

Chrissy opened her mouth to say something, but no words came out. Her gaze remained riveted on his equipment until she forced it up to his face.

His eyes glittered and Gareth took a step toward her, hands clenching and unclenching at his sides. He towered over her, his height intimidating as he invaded her personal space. Heat rolled off his body and a faint puff of air brushed her face when he whispered something in his guttural language. The ancient, foreign tongue sounded less harsh spoken in a quiet whisper. In fact, it sounded like a caress. "Hrun ni amberia."

"Oh," she said breathlessly.

Gareth encircled her wrist in his hand. "Hrun?"

Chrissy tilted her head back and looked up into his night-dark eyes. Her throat was dry despite the water she'd just swallowed. "Yes," she croaked, responding to the question in his voice.

He pulled her into the bedroom, pausing inside the darkened room to take her in his arms.

"Ni amberia." He bent his head and his mouth hovered inches from hers.

"I want you, too," she said before he kissed her.

His lips were soft in contrast to his hard, angular face. They teased hers open so his tongue could brush lightly against her lower lip. He angled his head and covered her mouth more fully, sweeping his tongue inside to meet hers. The heat and wetness of his mouth, hungrily possessing hers, ignited waves of fire inside her that licked through her whole body.

Chrissy stood on tiptoe, stretching against him to wrap her arms around his neck and kiss him fiercely. His hot, naked skin scorched her through the thin fabric of her T-shirt. His cock pressed against her belly, making her crotch ache with desire.

She rubbed herself against his erection and he groaned deep in his throat. Her pussy contracted, growing slippery wet at the erotic sound.

With his hands beneath her ass, Gareth lifted and carried her farther into her bedroom, kicking the door closed behind them. She gripped his shoulders, feeling the flow of muscle under his smooth skin. The sheer size and strength of him made her insides melt in a boneless puddle of want. The primitive desire to be possessed and filled reared up inside her, casually brushing away all reason and higher thinking.

He laid her on the unmade bed and she sprawled wantonly as though beseeching him to take her.

He straightened and looked down at her. Although she was still wearing a T-shirt and shorts, Chrissy already felt naked beneath his gaze.

This man was no cartoonish barbarian from the mists of history, but a living, breathing human being with a life he'd left behind that was as real as her own. Except his was over a thousand years past. How he must need her right now to verify he was still truly alive, when everything he knew was long dead.

She stripped off her T-shirt, wiggled out of her shorts and cast them on the floor. She extended her arms to Gareth. "Come."

He crawled onto the bed and over her waiting body, his weight supported by those massive arms. Lowering his body, he nudged at her opening with his heavy prick and began to push inside.

It was really happening. Too fast. Too soon.

"Wait!" Chrissy pressed her hands against Gareth's chest, feeling his heart pounding. "Not yet. I'm not ready."

He halted at her command, understanding the inflection of her words without the aid of a translator.

"Kiss me first," she commanded, reaching up to draw his face down to hers, showing him what she wanted. She pressed her lips against his, giving him soft, nibbling kisses and sucking at his full lower lip. She dipped her tongue in his mouth and teased his to response. Soon their tongues swirled together in a primal dance. Her hands tangled in the long, curling hair at his nape and cradled his skull, pulling him closer and deepening the kiss.

Gareth groaned low in his throat and started to push his cock inside her again.

She allowed it this time. His desperate need to enter touched her and foreplay probably wasn't included in primitive coupling. She could introduce him to more creative sex play when he wasn't so needy.

Chrissy was surprised to find she was actually ready for him. Her sex was slippery and aching, and when he filled her, she moaned in satisfaction. She briefly thought of the condoms in her nightstand drawer, but decided to forego them. He wasn't going to be carrying twenty-first century diseases, and she was on the pill so she didn't have to worry about getting pregnant. Besides, it felt so good to be sheathing a hot, thick cock with no latex membrane interfering. She clenched her inner muscles, gripping his shaft as it slid inside her.

Gareth's face drew into a scowl of concentration as he plunged into her. But when his eyes met hers, the frown disappeared. He smiled and murmured a foreign endearment that sounded sexy as hell, then leaned down to trail kisses from her mouth to her throat.

Running her hands from his broad shoulders down his satiny, naked back, she clutched his ass and pulled him even deeper. Her pussy stretched to accommodate his girth and the sensation of being completely filled was like eating a five-course meal after a long fast—utterly satisfying.

She reveled in his sheer, desperate hunger as he plunged recklessly inside her. Chrissy felt the edgy excitement of almost being out of control. She couldn't really stop him now if she wanted to and the sense of being in his power and relinquishing her own thrilled her.

The primitive love-making was so fast and intense. Gareth plunged into her with wild abandon, making the bed creak and tap against the wall hard enough to wake even Taylor. His face was buried against her shoulder. He grunted with each thrust and his cock head pushed against her very womb. Stroke after stroke, it was almost painful in its depth, yet pleasurable, too.

The combination of pleasure-pain built and built.

Her breasts mashed against Gareth's chest and her skin burned everywhere it slid against his. The heat grew inside her, embers fanning to flames until they exploded in a flash fire that consumed her. Chrissy moaned and cried out, arching her neck, her mouth falling open and long-suppressed cries of need pouring out.

Her hips arched off the bed to meet Gareth's final thrusts, then he, too, came with a shout. "Ai, gratchnya!" He gasped and spent deep inside her body.

Clutching his shoulders, she held on as he shuddered against her.

"Ai, amberia Kharissee. Ahh," he murmured into her hair.

Her eyes closed and she shivered at the exotic sound of his rumbling voice. The aftershocks of her orgasm settled to small pulses inside her like the flakes in a snowglobe settling after it's shaken.

"Mm," she whispered. "That was nice."

"Fircrantz un dian."

Gareth collapsed on Chrissy's body, out of his mind with ecstasy and unaware he was crushing her until she pushed against his chest. He murmured an apology and rolled onto his back beside her. A small corner of his mind noticed how soft yet firm the bed was. He'd never felt a sleeping mat so unbelievably comfortable. The rest of him was completely consumed with what had just transpired between him and this woman.

Desire for Chrissy had coursed through him since the moment he'd first touched her, flowing deep beneath his alarm at finding himself in a strange place. Part of his arousal had to do with the bloodlust stirred by the battle he'd been engaged in. Fighting always awoke his manhood and drove him to a frenzy of lust afterward. But beyond that he was attracted specifically to Chrissy, despite the beauty of the other two women in the house. Once more he considered the possibility she'd cast a spell over him. His reaction to her simply wasn't normal, so he must be bewitched.

Just now he'd rutted like an animal in heat, which also wasn't like him. Gareth knew how to satisfy a woman's needs and draw out her pleasure, but tonight he'd behaved like a lad of thirteen with his first woman. He'd plunged into Chrissy with no restraint, unable to stop his raging desire. He hadn't even tended to her breasts properly and they were a fine pair, small and round with ripe, red nipples that begged to be suckled and bitten. His behavior was humiliating and he wished she wore the translator so he could explain that he wasn't usually like this.

Turning his head on the soft pillow, he looked at her.

Her eyes were closed and she smiled.

Once more he felt the stirring of some enchantment deep inside him. He wanted her with a strange intensity the likes of which he'd never experienced. He needed to take her and possess her again, and he would...just as soon as he could move.

After a moment, Chrissy opened her eyes, looked at him and began to talk in her incomprehensible language. Without the device in his ear it sounded like, "Hour u du-win?" She rattled on for a bit as if he understood her.

Gareth let her musical voice flow over him. Her speech was much softer than his native tongue. He liked the way it sounded, like running water, and only wished he could understand.

"Teach me your words," he said slowly and distinctly. "What is this?" He held up the first thing that came to hand. It was the light, smooth, white cloth underneath the heavy, blue blanket. Gareth repeated as though talking to a young child, "What is this?"

Chrissy caught onto his questioning tone and answered, "Shect."

Gareth was excited. He dropped the sheet and grabbed the blanket. "And this?"

"Cum-fur-tur."

He smiled and repeated the words carefully. "Sheeth. Comfrtrrr." Then he held up his hand and looked at her with a raised brow.

"Hand." Chrissy smiled and he was amazed at how snowy white her teeth were. Every one of them stood in perfect alignment with the others.

Gareth pointed to his own teeth and received his next word.

"Teeth." She tapped hers then moved her finger to her lips and said, "Lips." She indicated her whole mouth with a little circle. "Mouth."

"Teezth, lips, moth." His hand descended to Chrissy's breast and began squeezing lightly. He looked at her through half-lidded eyes, smirking. "This?"

"Breast." She reached out and traced his nipple with the tip of her finger, sending shivers of lust through him. "Nipple." When he squirmed beneath her touch, she pinched his other nipple and repeated the word. "Nipple."

Gareth rose on one elbow and leaned down to take her nipple in his mouth. He licked the hard, rosy nub then lapped it into his mouth and sucked. Letting it go with a pop that jiggled her breast, he looked up at her. "Bresst." He squeezed the other one and pinched the rosy nub in the center. "Nibble."

Chrissy moaned and thrust her chest toward his hand.

He crawled up her body to lie over her, looking down into her eyes. "Ocu," he said, pointing to his eye.

"Eye," she told him.

He brushed his thumb just beneath her eye and when the lid fluttered closed, he kissed it. Then he tapped her nose. She named it and he kissed it. "Nuzz."

Caressing her soft lips with his finger, he struggled to recall the words she'd already taught him. "Lips. Moth." He gave her a long, lingering kiss then held up a handful of her long, auburn hair and let it sift through his fingers and fall across the pillow. "This?"

"Hair."

He burrowed his face in the sweet-smelling tresses, breathing in her sweet scent. "Heerr." Then he nibbled at her neck until she squirmed. He loved her full-throated laughter.

"Tickles," she said, pushing him away and pointing at the side of her neck. "Neck. Tickles."

Gareth kissed her throat, feeling her pulse throbbing.

"Throat." The word vibrated against his lips, tickling them.

He kissed her chest.

"Chest... Shoulders... Breasts... Ribs... Mmm. Stomach." She taught him the words as he moved his way down her anatomy. "Oh! Vagina—pussy."

"Poossay." He smiled as he opened the folds of her sex and licked her. Chrissy jerked and gasped at the touch of his tongue. Her musky scent and violent reaction made his cock stiffen again. He lapped deep inside her slit, tasting her juices and his own mingled together. Then he licked along her folds to the small, protruding bud where a woman's heart lay. A wise woman in his village had taught him all about the clitoris and how a man could make a woman beg for sex if he only took the time to tend it first. Gareth tickled Chrissy's pink pearl with the tip of his tongue then licked it with lingering, broad strokes.

She squirmed beneath his touch and moaned louder. Her hips thrust up toward his mouth, but Gareth held her down firmly while he had his way with her, teasing around her clitoris then attacking it again. He advanced and retreated again and again until the woman practically sobbed for relief.

"Oh, please," she moaned.

He smiled, recognizing entreaty when he heard it. Relenting, he nibbled her sensitive bud with careful teeth until she cried out and squirmed. Then he released his restraining hands on her hips and let her buck as she willed.

Chrissy arched her pelvis so high in the air her lower back and buttocks rose off the bed. Clenching the sheets on either side in her fists, she cried out and continued to jerk up and down as she came.

Gareth watched his handiwork with satisfaction. His erection throbbed hard and steady, pulsing in time to his heartbeats. Her moaning and writhing had him aching and ready again. Barely giving her time to recover from her orgasm, he rolled her onto her stomach, slipped a hand under her belly and hauled her up to her knees, then mounted her from behind.

Pinning her wrists to the bed on either side of her head, he drove inside her slowly, relishing the feel of her tight channel wrapping him like a glove. She was so wet and hot and the fit so close his cock registered every undulation of her inner muscles. He sucked in his breath with a hiss as sensations shivered up its length.

He gazed at the beautiful sight of Chrissy's tangled red tresses and the profile of her face on the white pillow, eyes closed, panting for breath. Her vulnerable neck, the long line of her spine and the soft curve of her ass tilted toward him made Gareth crave her with a fierce, aching desire.

Kneeling behind her, he gripped her waist and watched his glistening length withdraw from her depths. Her pussy made a slurping sound as it released him. Gareth held himself outside of her for several long seconds, quivering in anticipation, then plunged back into her delicious warmth. Her ass quivered at the force of his entry. Seeing his length swallowed inside her was entrancing and he simply watched his cock push in and pull out for several strokes.

"God, you feel so good!" Chrissy moaned into the pillow.

Gareth smiled at her pleasure and filled her again, strong and deep, ramming into her hard enough to move her up the bed. He grunted with satisfaction and his fingers dug into her hips.

"Harder," she commanded.

He took her word as encouragement and unleashed himself, pumping into her hard and fast, muttering low curses. The only sound in the quiet room besides his voice was the slap of flesh against flesh and Chrissy's soft moans. It was exhilarating being in the position of control over this lovely woman, especially since he hadn't felt in control of anything that had happened to him throughout the long, strange day.

Gareth thrust in and out a few more times, his balls tightening and his cock aching with tension, then he released, expending his seed deep inside her willing body. He roared his possession of her so loudly he knew the other women in the house must hear, but he didn't care. He wanted the world to know this woman was his now.

At the same moment, Chrissy lifted her ass toward him, accepting him completely. Her hips arched and she let out a low moan of fulfillment.

Gareth sighed and slumped over the soft body of the woman beneath him. Closing his eyes, he relaxed completely for several seconds then felt her stirring and rolled off her lest he crush her. He lay on his back in the soft, comfortable bed, staring at the shadowy shapes of strange furnishings in this foreign place and felt as if he'd come home. He had not been this content in a long time.

Turning his head, he looked at Chrissy.

She looked back at him with soft, unfocussed eyes and a smile. Her face was cast in light and shadow from the small glowing lamp on the wall.

Gareth patted her bottom and said, *"Ain,"* leaving his hand resting on her ass.

"Butt," Chrissy indicated her round buttocks. "Or ass."

Gareth understood she was naming the body part and he shook his head. "No. *Ain.*" He pointed first to himself and then to her making his possession clear. He looked into her eyes and repeated solemnly. *"Ain."*

"M-mine?" She swallowed. "Mine?"

He grunted and nodded. "Mine," he repeated emphatically.

He no longer cared if Chrissy was a witch. If he was under her spell, then let him remain so forever. He wanted her with every fiber of his being and didn't care if it was magic that made him feel that way. He would have her...again and again. And when the black witch finally found a way to send him home, he would take Chrissy with him.

Chapter Three

Lila sat slumped at her workstation, staring at the broken pieces of the time machine laid out before her. Moans and groans, a squeaking bed frame and loud cries drifted up through the register from the bedroom below. Damn, Chrissy! What part of "don't mess with the time traveler" didn't she understand? When Lila first became aware of the sounds rising from below, she thought Gareth was killing Chrissy. Her friend made whimpering sounds then let out a high-pitched cry. Lila suddenly realized it was a cry of ecstasy. Chrissy and the barbarian were having crazy, wild sex.

Lila hadn't been able to concentrate on her work since. The pair would quiet down for a little while then they'd be right back at it again. The frantic sounds of their coupling made her nipples ache. Her crotch pulsed in time with the banging headboard. Her hand sneaked down between her legs to give herself some relief, lightly rubbing her pussy through her clothing. It had been too damn long since she'd had a man. Her complete focus over the past year had been on this stupid machine—now lying broken before her in a thousand pieces.

The only man she'd talked to in weeks was MathMan, and that was just online chat. Lila didn't think of him as a real man, and they never talked about anything but theories and ideas. Yet now he was on his way to her house in the dead of night, coming to her rescue like a knight...or a creepy cyber-stalker. Lila suddenly realized she didn't even know his name. He'd always been MathMan. She had no idea what he looked like or what to expect, yet she'd given him her address without hesitation.

Lila supposed it was because she'd begun thinking of MathMan as a friend and confidante. He knew more about her plans and her current experiment than anyone else in her life. He was the only person she knew with a mind elastic enough to stretch around the concept underlying her time machine. She hadn't told him yet that her dreams had come to fruition in a machine that actually worked...when it wasn't broken.

"Ahhhh!" A protracted moan rose through the heat vent. Lila shivered and arched her pelvis forward into her hand. She gave in to her needs and slipped her hand inside her pants to rub her clit. Hissing with pleasure, she circled her finger round and round on the little nerve bundle until she was moaning like Chrissy.

Lila rocked back and forth in her seat, sending the wheels of the office chair rolling across the floor. Her eyes closed and she pictured her ideal man as she pleasured herself. Her dream lover was tall, broad-shouldered with dark coffee skin, chocolate eyes and a sinful smile that flashed white teeth and dimples. His smooth, muscular body was sculpted like an ebony statue.

She ran her tongue over her lips and moaned louder. Her other hand slid underneath her shirt and bra and began squeezing her tit and pinching her nipple. The man in her daydream did the same. She rocked her hips as the friction of her finger sent jolts of electricity coursing through her. The chair rolled another foot backward across the floor.

Suddenly the doorbell rang. Lila jumped and almost fell off her chair. "Shit!" She pulled her hands out of her pants and from under her shirt then raced down two flights of stairs to the front door. She arrived breathless and sweating, forgot to check the peephole and swung the door open at one-thirty in the morning to let a virtual stranger in her house.

MathMan was tall, towering over her by almost a head, and she was not a petite woman. But in no other respect did he resemble her dream man. He was long and lanky with no powerful muscles straining his shirt. His shaggy, dirty-blond hair stuck up in random tufts around his fine-boned face. His nose and lips were thin and his jaw long. It was too dark to discern his eye color, but they were wide and pale. Pale like his skin, which glowed whitely in the streetlight.

"MathMan?" she asked.

"Yeah. Zach, actually." He grinned as he stuck out his hand and enveloped hers in a firm grip. "Glad to finally meet you." Dimples flashed.

Lila stared. He had the dimples. She shook herself and smiled back. "Hi, I'm Lila."

"Lila," he repeated, and his goofy smile widened. "Pretty name for a pretty girl."

"Please, you did not just say that." She raised an eyebrow.

"Sorry. Lame. I just..." He flailed his hand around as though trying to pluck words from the air. "It's weird meeting you in person like this. We've talked for so long, but I didn't think we were ever going to finally meet."

"And yet, here we are," she said dryly. "So are you going to come in and help me work this problem or what?"

"Oh. Sure."

Lila stood back to let Zach in and noticed he ducked his head slightly when entering the doorway. He reminded her of a giraffe or maybe a crane, something with long, awkward limbs and an ungainly gate.

She glanced at his big, bony hands, easily large enough to span a woman's waist...well, maybe not any woman's, but hers for sure, and wondered what that would feel like.

"Thanks for coming," she said, suddenly remembering her manners. "Sorry if I was rude just now. I can't think straight anymore."

Zach followed her toward the stairs. "You know how it goes. Take a break from the problem and it'll practically solve itself. You just need to rest then come back at it with your head clear."

"I don't have that luxury. This is kind of a time-sensitive situation."

They reached the second floor landing. When Lila turned to address him, he was right behind her and she bumped into him. She stepped back quickly, looking up into his eyes—a kind of translucent green, it turned out. Hypnotizing eyes, actually. They were clear and guileless, framed in long, thick eyelashes that made them look larger than they were.

Zach blinked and the spell was broken.

"Huh." Lila jump-started her mouth. "Yeah, anyway, the point is I can't afford to rest. I've got to solve this thing, tonight if possible." She turned and led him up the last flight of stairs to her domain on the third floor. She paused at the door, hand on the knob. "This invention is going to sound... You might have trouble believing... Remember all the times we talked about time travel, the possible ways of accomplishing it and the ramifications if it were possible? This is going to seem crazy but..."

He touched her arm. "Just show me."

The skin of her forearm tingled after he moved his hand away. Lila took a deep breath. "All right." She opened the door.

Zach walked into the room and over to the time machine.

Seeing it through his eyes, Lila admitted the cubicle had a very *Bill and Ted's Excellent Adventure* vibe. "That's the transporting station," she explained. "The machine itself is over here." She gestured Zach toward her workstation where the mangled computer guts were spilled.

He approached the table and began examining parts, silent while he scanned everything, clearly processing information and trying to assimilate it. "What exactly am I looking at here? Is this...what we've talked about?"

Lila nodded, almost holding her breath while she waited for his reaction.

"Time travel," he murmured, running his hand over the creased schematic Lila had pinned on the bulletin board above the table. His finger traced the diagram. When he turned to her without a smile on his face, she knew he believed. "Explain," he ordered.

Lila was struck by the intensity of his eyes. The aw-shucks, goofy guy on the front porch had transformed into a serious, focused man. Even with his long, floppy hair and bangs in his eyes, Zach didn't look like a boy anymore. With his brow furrowed and his wide mouth thinned to a straight line, he seemed older, his youthful awkwardness gone. Her pulse quickened under his steady gaze and she licked her lips and began to outline her project. "It works like this..."

A half hour and a steady barrage of Zach's questions later, Lila completed her explanation.

There were several moments of silence during which he continued to stare from the schematic to the parts on the bench and back, then he said in an awed tone, "You did it. All that talk... I thought we were hypothesizing, but you really did it." There wasn't a trace of doubt in his voice.

"And now I have to undo it," Lila said dryly, then added, "Thanks for believing me." It warmed her heart that Zach trusted her without even seeing the machine demonstrated or meeting Gareth—although producing a man and calling him an ancient barbarian didn't make it so. Any actor could play the part. "You're taking a lot on faith."

"It's not faith. I can see how it works." He gestured at the worn, coffee-stained schematic. "Your plan is flawless, and..." He shook his head. "Actually fucking amazing." He looked at her again with those pale emerald eyes that caught the light and reflected it brightly. "You're brilliant."

Lila's heart warmed even more...or maybe it was her blood. The room seemed suddenly hot. A flush burned in her cheeks at the compliment and she wished he'd quit looking at her. It made her insides feel all squishy. "Thanks." She looked down at the workbench and began fiddling with a piece of broken plastic.

Zach clapped his hands together, making her jump. "So let's get started. We'll work this step by step until we get it all back together and working again."

Lila felt a brief rush of annoyance at his take-charge attitude, but also relief because her mind was numb from running in circles for the past eight hours. "Can I get you a cup of coffee or something to eat first?"

"Sure. Caffeine me up, Scotty." His voice was overly hearty and he blushed when she stared at him. "Yes, please," he amended.

Just when she was starting to think he was kind of cute, he showed his inner geek. Lila walked from the room mentally shaking her head.

Caffeine me up, Scotty? Where the hell had that come from? Zach winced the moment the silly words were out of his mouth. Why did beautiful girls always have this effect on him? He tried too hard to be witty and only ended up saying lame things like that. *Pretty name for a pretty girl?* God, what he needed was a Cyrano to write his dialogue for him and feed it to him over a headset.

Lila was so much more than Zach had expected. In their conversations throughout the last year and a half he'd come to admire her enormous intellect, but since they'd never web-cammed or uploaded pictures, he hadn't known what to expect in the looks department before tonight. Lila was a stunner and way out of his league. He was amazed he'd been able to squeeze any words past his tongue at all from the moment she'd opened the door and he beheld her incredible gorgeousness.

"Asshole. Asshole. Asshole. Think before you speak," he whispered urgently to himself after he heard her descend the stairs. "Calm down and talk to her like an equal, like you've always done online. It's about the science, man." *Not her amazing breasts and mouth-*

watering ass and those fantastic brown eyes that freeze your brain and stir your cock.

Zach sat in Lila's swivel office chair and spun back and forth, staring at the litter of the computer terminal. This project was mind-boggling and so were the possible consequences of time travel. Even if he could help Lila get the machine back together and functional again, he didn't know if this was technology she should share with the world. After they sent this Gareth guy she'd told him about back where he belonged, they should probably destroy the thing. God, he couldn't wait to meet the guy, to see for himself a living fragment of history—a time traveler.

Could this night get any stranger? He'd been summoned in the middle of the night by the woman of his dreams to come to her aid like a knight in shining armor. Then he'd found out Lila wasn't the sweet-faced, little computer nerd he'd pictured, but a statuesque, beautiful, brilliant woman—who, incidentally, had created then broken a time machine and needed his help in putting it back together. This was the kind of scenario sci-fi geeks like him only daydreamed about.

A few moments later, Lila returned with two steaming cups of coffee. "Listen, I want to apologize again for being short with you earlier when I should have been thanking you for driving all the way here. You got here a lot faster than I expected."

"It only took an hour and a half. No big deal." He accepted the coffee. "Thanks. The truth is I've wanted to get together for a long time, but I thought you'd think I was creepy if I asked to meet."

Lila smiled and Zach's heart liquefied. "No, not at all. We've been friends for almost two years now. It's about time we met in person. You know more about my work and my hopes and dreams than anybody."

Zach could feel some stupid, inane comment bubbling up and about to spout forth from his mouth so he quickly turned his attention back to the broken terminal. "Well, let's get started."

"Okay." Lila pulled up another chair beside him. She sat so close he could smell her perfume or maybe it was her deodorant or shampoo—something sweet, floral and feminine. The pretty scent and the heat of her body next to him made it hard to concentrate at first, but then Zach became entranced by the ingeniousness of her invention and almost forgot about the woman beside him.

Together they worked on re-configuring the terminal and cataloging which parts would need replacement. Zach even had some suggestions for improvements, a more streamlined approach to Lila's design.

Suddenly he became aware of the sound of low moans and answering groans floating into the room from the heat duct in the wall. Zach paused in the middle of his calculations. "Is that...?" He blushed and stopped speaking as it became clear the sounds were exactly what he thought they were, a couple having sex.

Lila sighed, tossed her pen down and leaned back in her chair. "Yes, it is. My roommate, Chrissy, and the barbarian guy, Gareth, having sex. Can you believe it? I told these girls to keep him as insulated as possible from everything in the modern world so when I send him back, he won't be tainted by contact with our time. He might bring back knowledge that would change the entire course of history."

"Considering what they're doing, I doubt he's learning anything he didn't know before," Zach said. "And when we talked about the butterfly effect, didn't we decide that whatever changes a person made in the past, it wouldn't matter—"

"Because that's the way the course of history was meant to be," Lila completed. "Yeah, that's what *you* said. But I'm not so sure, and I don't want to test it. I don't want to be the person who plays games with time and ends up bringing doom to the human race."

An especially loud male groan rose from the register and Zach smiled. "I don't think a little harmless sex is going to bring about either a Utopian society or a new Third Reich."

Both of them fell silent for a moment listening to Chrissy cry out, "Oh God. Gareth! Oh God! Mmmm."

Zach shifted in his chair, crossing his legs to hide his growing erection. "So this Gareth guy doesn't have questionable hygiene and rotten teeth, I take it?"

"No." Lila picked up her pen and fiddled with it, clicking it nervously in and out. "He cleaned up really well, actually. My other roommate, Taylor, cut his hair and trimmed his beard, also interfering with history.

When we send him back, how will Gareth explain his new appearance? And I have to pinpoint the exact moment from which I took him and return him there." Lila sighed and clicked her pen hard. "Hell, I'm afraid it'll be all I can do just to get him in the right year, let alone the right moment. I'm afraid I really screwed up here, Zach."

From below came a hoarse male cry. "Ai, Kharissee! Unhhhh."

Zach swallowed hard as he listened to the man's orgasm. He closed his eyes a second and willed his penis down then turned to Lila. "It's all right. Don't sweat it. Everything will turn out okay."

Tears glittered in Lila's eyes. She brushed them away and sniffed. "Damn, I'm a nervous wreck."

Zach stood, stepped behind her and put his hands on her shoulders, feeling the tense muscles cording her neck and shoulders as he massaged. At first she stiffened under his touch, but then relaxed bit by bit, letting his hands pull the knots of tension loose.

"Relax," he said quietly. "We'll work this problem together. Panicking won't solve anything, just relax." He dug his fingers quite hard into her upper back, massaging between her shoulder blades then slid his hands up the long, beautiful column of her neck and gently stroked the stiffness from it. Her skin was warm and soft under his fingers.

Lila stretched and moaned. "Ah, that feels so good."

Zach's cock grew harder. Her soft moan sounded too similar to the orgasmic cries from below, which had finally died down to silence. He pictured Lila in the throes of passion, writhing on rumpled sheets beneath him, her eyes closed and mouth open, gasping out his name. He could imagine it all too well and felt like a perv giving her a massage while his steadily growing boner loomed between them. He patted her shoulders and returned to his chair, leaning forward as though to study the schematic again. "Guess we should get back to it."

"Oh. Yeah." Lila seemed flustered. She dropped the pen she'd been playing with, leaned to pick it up and bumped her forehead against the edge of the work station on the way down. "Ouch!" She rubbed her head.

"You okay?" Zach looked at her and swore Lila was blushing under her deep brown skin. Could a phenomenal woman like her possibly be flustered because of him? No way. It was wishful thinking.

"I'm fine," she said shortly. "You're right. Let's get back to work."

A few hours and a pounding headache later, Zach picked up the two tiny units he'd been trying to fit together and threw them across the table. "This is bullshit. I can't fix this. We have to order more of these, too."

"No duh," Lila snapped. "I tried to tell you that twenty minutes ago, but you wouldn't listen."

Zach glared at her. She looked less enticing and more like a bitch as each frustrating minute slipped past. Nothing worked the way it was supposed to and the pair of them couldn't agree on anything. Zach generally considered himself an easy-going guy, but Lila was bringing out the worst in him. "I need a bathroom break. Where is it?"

"Second floor, the door at the end of the hall." Lila's attention was back on her work and she didn't even bother to get up and show him the way.

Zach descended the stairs, fuming. Here he'd come to help her out and she was treating him like a pest who was getting in her way. Ungrateful bitch. He walked down the shadowy hall toward the bathroom. A light showed at the bottom of the door and Zach waited in the hall for the occupant to emerge, hoping he wouldn't catch one of Lila's housemates unaware and freak her out. He stayed several respectful yards away from the door waiting his turn.

When the bathroom door opened, the broad-shouldered silhouette of a half-naked man stood in the brightly lit rectangle.

Zach's eyes widened at the sight of the time-traveling barbarian. He barely had time to process who it was before the big man came barreling down the hall, threw him up against the wall and pinned him with a forearm against his throat.

Feet dangling above the floor, Zach gasped for air. "Hey, man," he croaked, trying to grab the thick arm crushing his windpipe. "It's okay. Back off."

"Schiagrovia mecklin?" the man shouted, his eyes narrowed in suspicion. He shoved Zach against the wall even harder, pinning him with his heavy body clothed only in a pair of boxer briefs.

Zach was probably a head taller than the time-traveler, but Gareth was bulky with muscle and outweighed him by a good forty pounds. Besides which, Zach had never been in a fight in his entire life unless one included getting beaten up on the playground a few times in elementary school. "I don't know," he answered the unintelligible question. He struggled to raise his hands to show his surrender, but they were trapped against the wall by Gareth's torso. "Let me down."

Slowly Gareth released his hold, letting Zach slide down the wall until he was on his feet again. The warrior backed off a step, taking his arm away, but clearly ready to apply pressure again if he made any sudden moves.

Rubbing his throat, Zach coughed and drew in a deep breath of air, smelling the musky odor of sex emanating from the man. Adrenaline coursing through his body left it shaky and at the same time perversely horny as he remembered the erotic sounds that had drifted up through the grate.

Just then, a woman with tangled red hair burst out of the door next to the bathroom. She was wrapped in a sheet and, Zach deduced from her naked shoulders, nothing else. When she saw him, she froze. "Oh my God, who are you?"

"Lila's friend, Zach. She called me to come help with your situation here." Zach nodded at Gareth. "You must be Chrissy."

Lila clattered down the stairs from the third floor and flipped on the hall light making all of them wince and squint. "What's going on? What happened?"

"Your barbarian just tried to kill me," Zach snapped, feeling unaccountably irritated with Lila. She was looking at him as if *he'd* done something wrong.

"Mecklin," Gareth snarled, taking a menacing step toward him.

"Whatever, dude." Zach straightened to his full height and tried not to look intimidated.

Chrissy approached Zach. "Are you all right? I'm so sorry about that," she said as though her dog had escaped its leash and attacked a neighbor.

Gareth stepped between them, turning to the half-clothed woman and gesturing toward the bedroom. "Friste enlar," he ordered.

"Don't tell me what to do!" Chrissy frowned.

"Everybody calm down." Lila approached the trio and spoke to Zach. "Gareth doesn't know any better. He probably thought you were an intruder. Why don't you go back upstairs? Chrissy, get your caveman boyfriend under control. Make him wear his translator, for God's sake, so he knows what's going on. I know sex is the universal language, but don't be ridiculous."

"That's love," Zach corrected. "Love is the universal language."

Lila glared at him. "Whatever!" She turned her attention to Gareth. "And you...chill out. We're doing everything we can to get you back home again, all right?"

Gareth frowned. "Zgradia."

Lila sighed and shook her head. "Never mind. Just get him back to bed, Chrissy."

"Chrissy, ain." Gareth declared.

"No, I'm not yours," she protested and turned beseechingly to Lila. "He thinks we're wed now or something. What am I going to do?"

"Shoulda thought of that before you let him in your pants," Lila snapped unsympathetically. "Get the damn translator back on and explain that you're not."

Zach turned to head upstairs then realized he'd never had the chance to pee, and needed to more than ever after his alarming experience. "Hey. I'll catch up with you. I've gotta..." He nodded toward the bathroom. He didn't take his eyes off Gareth as he walked cautiously past him.

The warrior met his gaze. "Lila, tura?" Gareth gestured back and forth between Lila and Zach. "Tura?" he repeated with a questioning lift of his eyebrows.

"No, man, she's definitely not mine." Zach walked into the bathroom and closed the door behind him.

Lila retreated back upstairs, ridiculously flustered by Gareth's assumption that she and Zach were an item. Why in the world did it bother her so much? Maybe because the idea wasn't completely unwelcome. Throughout the evening she'd found her computer buddy sexier than she wanted to. Zach might not have a testosterone-fueled physique, but she could imagine that long, lean body wrapped around her. His face was attractive in a genial, boy-next-door kind of way. And his eyes...were riveting. They were the fresh green of new leaves and fringed by thick, brown lashes that would feel incredible batting against a person's skin in a butterfly kiss.

"Shut up," Lila murmured to her libido. She sat down at her laptop, called up the site from which she ordered components and began placing her order. By the time she'd chosen Fed-Ex twenty-four-hour delivery and snapped her notebook closed, Zach was back. Lila spun around on her chair to face him. "Hey, sorry about you getting attacked."

He shrugged. "It's okay. No harm done."

"I don't think Gareth's dangerous. You just startled him."

"I know. And threatened his woman." He gave a lopsided smile and leaned against the desk next to her, his long legs crossed before him. "When I got done peeing my pants about being choked and actually processed the fact the man is from the past... I mean, wow, time travel! I can hardly believe it. And those translating devices? Absolute genius! How did you come up with them?"

"Something you said during one of our chats. Trying to translate language word for word makes zero sense, but transmitting a visual concept from one brain to another—that's logical. It was actually easier to make than you would expect." Lila proceeded to explain the process.

Zach nodded, perfectly in sync with her idea. He punctuated her words with "Of course" and "Absolutely." And when she was finished, he exclaimed, "Genius!" again.

His appreciative reaction warmed and pleased her. She'd kept her work to herself for so long it felt wonderful to share everything with someone who understood. "Well." She stood. "We should get some rest."

"Oh...yeah... I should probably get going." Pushing off the desk, he straightened and glanced past her toward the door.

"Or you could rest here. I don't want you driving home and falling asleep at the wheel." Lila flushed. "Unless there's something you have to do tomorrow, you could hang around until the parts come in and..."

"I'd love to help. Not that I did much tonight."

"Yes, you did." She impulsively took his hand. "Just having you here was a big help. I felt so overwhelmed and when you arrived you gave me a fresh burst of confidence. I couldn't have made it through tonight without you. Thanks."

He smiled. The dimples flashed.

Her heart flipped. She cleared her throat and let go of his warm hand. "I'll make a pallet on the floor here if that's okay. Unless...maybe you'd rather sleep down on the couch. I don't think you have anything to worry about from Gareth."

"No," Zach said quickly. "Here's fine."

"All right then."

After using the bathroom and getting a pile of cushions, blankets and pillows, Lila climbed the stairs to her attic room once more. She was exhausted. It felt like this had been the longest day of her life and when she checked her watch she realized that was because it was the next morning. Four-thirty.

"I hope you'll be comfortable," she said as she arranged the cushions for Zach and covered them with linens and blankets. "Sorry we don't have any sleeping bags."

"It's great," he said.

Lila straightened and froze for a second.

Zach had taken off his flannel shirt and was wearing only his T-shirt. The biceps it revealed were much more sculpted than Lila had expected—not beefy, but sinewy. His jeans hung low on his narrow hips, revealing an inch of white underwear. When Zach lifted his arms to stretch and yawn, Lila glimpsed flat stomach and a trail of hair leading from his navel down to the fly of his pants. His body was long, lean and graceful...not gawky after all.

He glanced at her and caught her staring at his torso.

Lila quickly turned away and walked toward her dresser. It was a pain to have her workplace and bedroom all in one space, making it hard to sleep sometimes when her brain was really revved up over a new idea. But she'd learned to separate work and relaxation and the bedroom half of the open loft reflected her traditional tastes. The piece of carpet she'd placed to delineate the area was a deep royal blue. The furniture was a mix of periods, but all antiques. She'd lovingly shoved the heavy bureau and pieces of bed up two flights of stairs much to the moaning dismay of her helpers, Chrissy and Taylor. The bed was covered with a colorful wedding ring quilt, the showpiece of her little room.

"Could you, um, look the other way for a minute?" she asked Zach.

He obliged.

She took a good look at his blue jeans-clad ass and the long line of his back then stripped and pulled on a tank top and sweatpants. "Okay." She walked past Zach to turn off the light and felt his eyes watching her in her skimpy top and loose pants. At least, she thought he was looking, but when she glanced over her shoulder, he was pulling back the covers of his makeshift bed to lie down. She must be transferring her own fevered longings onto him.

Lila turned off the light then re-crossed the room and climbed into bed. Her pulse and her mind raced a mile a minute both from the day's stress and from having Zach lying on her floor. She didn't think she'd ever be able to sleep. She rolled over with her back toward him. "'Night."

"Goodnight." His low, disembodied voice drifted through the dark room.

It made her feel warm and safe. Actually more hot than warm and more aroused than safe, but close enough. Despite her doubts and worries, she fell asleep in only a few minutes.

Chapter Four

Chrissy woke from a dream in which she was wrapped in the embrace of a giant black bear. Her eyes flew open, but the snuffling breathing in her ear didn't stop, the big arms clasping her didn't disappear and the tickling fur against her shoulder kept on tickling.

Gareth's face was nestled into the curve of the back of her neck. His muscular arm draped over her body and his naked leg wrapped possessively around hers. His morning erection pressed between her ass cheeks. Good God, the man had stamina. She wouldn't have imagined he was capable of another hard-on after last night.

Last night. She winced and sucked in a breath through her teeth. Had she really done all that? And why? Oh right, because it felt so damn good at the time. Seriously, what had she been thinking having sex—repeatedly—with this primitive man? It was so wrong and could lead nowhere. But although she and Gareth could barely communicate, Chrissy had felt more of a connection with him than with any of the guys she'd ever dated, which was frightening. Inexplicable and frightening.

He moaned and murmured something then rolled away from her, releasing her from the grip of his heavy arm.

She crept out of the warm bed and stood beside it a moment looking at the ripped abs and massive biceps of the sleeping man. She gazed at his black eyelashes fanned against his cheeks, the strong jaw emphasized by the fringe of beard and generous lips accented by his moustache. Damn, Taylor had done a good barbering job. Gareth was absolutely stunning.

Tearing herself away from the memory of how that facial hair felt tickling her inner thighs, she headed for the bathroom to shower. She felt like the smell of sex was oozing out of her every pore and stood under the steaming spray for a long time. When she returned to her room, clean and moist and wrapped in a towel, Gareth was awake.

He lay on his back, arms behind his head, his nude body provocatively displayed, and grinned at her. "Barndia en hach, Chrissy?" Removing one hand from behind his head, he stroked the hard length of his cock enticingly. "Ragrarran?" He rolled his r's in a suggestive rumble.

"Uh, no. Not again." Chrissy forced her gaze away. His deep, cajoling voice was as seductive as his body. "I have to go... Hold on a sec." She raised a finger before trotting out of the room. She went to Taylor's room, glad it was empty because she didn't want to deal with her teasing, and got the translator from the nightstand. Placing it in her ear, she returned to Gareth and motioned for him to do the same. When his translator was in place she said, "I'm going out for a run. I'll be back soon."

"Run?" He sat up, watching her put on her tennis shoes.

"Yeah. In the park." Chrissy glanced at him, careful to focus on his face and not his still-straining cock.

"Why do you run?" A puzzled frown creased his forehead.

She tried to imagine how strange it would seem to someone from his time to run for no other reason than the pleasure of it. "Exercise. To keep my body fit."

He gave her a long look from head to toe as she stood. "You are already fit. Very fit."

"Yeah, because I run. My job doesn't allow me much time to get outdoors and move around."

"What is your job?" He moved to the edge of the bed, his long legs stretching to the floor.

"I work at a bank. That's a place where people's money is kept safe. My job is a loan officer. I decide who can borrow money from the bank."

Gareth stared at her blankly. "Borrow money from the other people?"

Chrissy sighed. "It's kind of complicated and I'll explain it to you later, but right now I want to go on my run." She gathered her hair into a ponytail and slipped an elastic band around it.

Gareth stood up. "All right. I will run with you."

"Oh." The last thing she wanted was Gareth's company. She needed to get away from this man and regain some perspective, but she couldn't find a way to tell him no. "Fine. Get dressed. I'll wait for you down in the kitchen." She turned to go.

"Come here first," Gareth ordered, reaching out to her. "Come."

She couldn't resist his extended hand and walked over to him. He enfolded her in his hard embrace, pressing her against his over-heated body. "The sex last night was very good." He kissed the top of her head and played with her damp ponytail. "We should have more now."

Chrissy pushed against his chest and wriggled out of his grip. "Maybe later. Run first." She quickly left the room.

"Good God, I've created a monster," she whispered to herself as she hurried downstairs.

Taylor was in the kitchen, leaning against the counter eating a Poptart and looking at an issue of *Cosmo*. She looked up with a mischievous grin when Chrissy entered the room. "Hey, hellcat, I heard you going at it last night. Man, you were a wild woman. I had to take a sleeping pill and wear my iPod headphones to get any sleep and even then I had erotic dreams all night. Do you ever have the one where a guy makes you come just by licking your toes?" She waited for Chrissy's answer with an expectant look and when she didn't reply, Taylor shrugged. "No? Just me then, I guess."

"I'm sorry about...the noise." Chrissy felt her cheeks flaming. "I didn't mean to get so, uh, carried away."

"It's good for you. You should do it more often." Taylor popped the last bit of pastry into her mouth.

Chrissy exhaled loudly. "I had no idea I was going to...I didn't mean for this to happen. Gareth's not like..."

"Not like what? Not like supremely hot and pumped full of juicy male hormones? I'd do him."

"It's almost like he's a child in our world. I feel like I took advantage of him, like I shouldn't be messing with someone so innocent."

"Didn't sound innocent to me last night. I think he handled it just fine." She closed her magazine and tossed it on the kitchen table. "Jeez, you're such a worrier. You and Lila. How'd I end up rooming with you two neurotic chicks?"

Chrissy listened for Gareth, then leaned forward and lowered her voice. "I think he has a crush on me. He keeps calling me 'his' and acting attached, like we have some kind of bond now. What should I do?"

"'His'? Sounds sexy, very caveman-possessive." Taylor mock-shivered and grinned. "Lucky you."

"Stop it. It's not funny. I think this is going to end very badly. What do you think a barbarian does when he wants something? He takes it. And what's going to happen when he realizes he can't have me?"

Taylor had no chance to reply before Gareth entered the room. He was dressed in the same shirt and jeans from yesterday, not really suitable clothes for a jog. "Hello, Tay-lorr," he rumbled.

"He says, 'hello'," Chrissy translated since Taylor wasn't wearing a translator.

"Yeah. Kinda got that. Look, guys, I've gotta split for work. I've got a shift today. See you later. Enjoy your run and anything else you find to do today." She winked and bounced out of the kitchen.

"What kind of work does she do?" Gareth asked.

"Taylor is a physical therapist. Um, that's someone who helps people recover after they've been sick."

"Ah, a healer." He nodded. "And the dark witch, Lila? What is her purpose? Why does she conjure people through time?"

"She didn't conjure you. It's not magic like you're thinking. Lila is a lab technician. That's her day job, when she's working, but she's really an inventor. What she used to bring you here was a machine she invented, not magic."

"What about her lover? What does he do?"

"Lover?" For a moment Chrissy was at a loss. "Oh, Zach. He's one of her online friends. She called him to come and help with the time machine." Reminding Gareth he was stranded here didn't seem like a good idea. "Look, we can talk later, but first—"

"We run," he supplied.

"Yes."

The sun burned down hot, making Gareth's shirt stick between his shoulder blades as he jogged alongside Chrissy. He glanced over at her tits bouncing up and down slightly in the halter contraption that held them in place. It was an ingenious device. He imagined it kept a woman's breasts high and firm long after her youth. Perhaps when he returned home with Chrissy she could show the other women in the village how to sew something like that.

He looked around at the tall trees, green grass and colorful flower beds in the park. It was hard to believe how bereft he'd felt here yesterday. With Chrissy running by his side, the park seemed a beautiful place. He hoped she would be happy living with him. She would have to be, because, after last night, he was not going to let her go.

Gareth tried to picture her drawing water from the village well, feeding pigs, sweeping out the hearth or tanning hides with the other women. None of these pictures would come into focus. A shadow of doubt about his plan crept into his mind. Women were often taken as spoils of war and eventually settled into village life, but somehow he knew Chrissy was too different. Taking her home with him would be like forcing a dove to live among starlings.

"There's a café across from the park just up ahead," she panted as she ran. "We can stop there for brunch." She slowed from a jog to a trot to a walk.

Gareth kept pace with her.

She put two fingers on her pulse then looked at a gadget on her wrist. When she wiped her forearm across her sweaty forehead, the scent of her body wafted to Gareth, making him hard.

He grabbed her hand and pulled her off the smooth black path into the trees. "Come."

"What? I—"

He cut off her words with a kiss, lifting her and pressing her back against a wide, gray tree trunk. His tongue plunged into her mouth, finding hers and stroking it. His hands cupped her bottom and pulled her tight against him.

Chrissy made a small, soft sound and her arms went around his neck, holding on tight.

Gareth moved his mouth from her lips to her throat, licking up and down the long, white column, tasting delicious salt. He squeezed the soft mound of her breast through the gray fabric of her top.

Arching into his hand, she quivered as his tongue licked the hollow of her throat. "Oh, no. Not here," she murmured.

He moved his head down until his mouth enveloped her tit, wetting the material and making her nipple bead sharply. He sucked hard, pulling the bud into his mouth and rolling his tongue over it.

She gasped. Her hands plunged into his hair and held his head.

He didn't know if she was trying to force him away or pull him closer.

"Stop," she begged weakly.

He raised his head to kiss her mouth again and pressed his erection into her crotch, rubbing against her.

They kissed desperately, feverishly for several more minutes under the sheltering tree, then Chrissy pulled away with a gasp and pushed hard on his chest. "Enough! Seriously. Let's go get breakfast."

Gareth chuckled and put her down, setting her gently back on her feet, then followed her back to the jogging path.

The place Chrissy took him was clean and brightly lit. There were only a few customers sitting at small tables. It was nothing like the dark, crowded alehouse at home. As Chrissy ordered food, he looked around for the source of the soft music playing in the room, but could find no musicians.

She led him outdoors to a table where they ate the foods she'd chosen for them. Gareth found the eggs delicious. They were spiced with herbs he didn't recognize and sprinkled with some kind of cheese. The toasted bread was delicate and crisp, nothing like the hearty brown loaves he was used to. He tasted the bright yellow juice Chrissy recommended and found it both tart and sweet at the same time. It was like sunshine in his mouth.

He finished all of his food quickly and she ordered more for him. Gareth continued to eat long after Chrissy had finished and sat sipping her cup of the bitter beverage called "cawfee".

"So, Gareth, tell me about yourself. What is your village called? How many people live there? What do you do for a living?"

"My town is Cuildwen. Between the village and surrounding farms there are..." He calculated. "Over two hundred people. I own a forge."

"So you're a blacksmith and a warrior."

Gareth bit into a piece of crisp bacon. "The people in my village are mostly farmers and craftsmen. When we're attacked, someone must defend. I've had experience in warfare and so I lead."

"What about your family, parents, siblings? Do you have a...wife or girlfriend?"

A slow smile crept across his face and he answered her last question first. "No. I have no woman in my life."

Chrissy's gaze dropped from his and a pretty pink flush colored her cheeks. She cleared her throat. "Tell me about your family."

"My mother died giving birth to my youngest brother. Father drowned while fishing. There were ten of us children. Some are grown and married with families of their own. Two of my brothers died as infants, and Alian, Morgrav and Cyrrga died last year from an illness that swept the village. The younger children are being raised by my aunts and older sisters."

"I'm sorry." Chrissy's voice was soft. "It must have been very hard to lose so much of your family like that."

Gareth grunted. There was nothing he could say about the bleak years when one after another of his family

89

members had slipped away. "I didn't want to stay in the village and live the same life my parents had, so I left the village and traveled, for a while. I learned to fight as a mercenary, helping whoever paid me, and when I returned home after a number of years, it fell to me to organize the men to stand against the invaders from the north."

"There were no government forces to fight off the invaders?"

He shook his head, looking surprised at the idea.

"So, every village for itself."

"Yes." Gareth frowned. "Who protects your lands?"

"National armed forces. They're paid soldiers serving the entire country."

"Mercenaries," he clarified.

"I guess, but not exactly like that, either. A lot has changed in the world since your time."

"Tell me." Gareth put his fork down, laced his hands together and leaned forward eager to learn.

Chrissy inhaled. "I hardly know where to begin there's so much to cover. Here's the short version. People discovered new lands, new technology and invented things to make life easier, but humans still make stupid mistakes, fall in love, have families, fight each other, live and die just like always. There are still wars over land and religion." She gestured at the tall buildings rising around them. "Despite appearances, it's the same old world."

He nodded. It was kind of comforting to hear. "What about your family? Is it large?"

"No. Just my parents and me, plus a few aunts, uncles and cousins. Being an only child made me kind of the total focus of their attention, especially my mom. I think she felt since she only had one canvas to work on, she'd better make the painting perfect."

He shook his head, understanding the words but not her meaning.

"Hypercritical. I can never please her no matter what I do. Took me a long time to realize it, but I finally did and now I don't try." She laughed, but there was no humor in it. "We have a truce, but not the warmest relationship."

Gareth didn't know what to say. He'd never heard anyone talk about their feelings about their parents. A family was part of who you were and there was nothing more to say about it. Uncomfortable at her openness, he changed the subject. "You are an unmarried woman, yet you don't live with your parents. Are you and your friends widows?"

Her laughter was genuine this time. "No. Many single women live on their own nowadays. It's not necessary to have a man to, uh, take care of us anymore. We hold jobs of our own, earn our own money, make our own way in the world."

"That is good."

"Huh. I thought you'd think a woman's place was in the home. Maybe you're not such a barbarian after all."

He could tell from her tone she was teasing, but he didn't quite understand the joke. "I have seen old women forced to live on the charity of others when they outlived their spouses and even their sons. I always thought they should be able to earn enough from weaving or washing or baking to keep them comfortably." Gareth looked deeply into her eyes and, although he smiled, he was serious as he said, "Perhaps you will come back with me and show the women in my village a new way to do things."

Chrissy shook her head. "No, Gareth. You must know it's not possible for me to go home with you. I couldn't live that way, not knowing everything I know. It would be too hard. I don't have any of the necessary skills to survive in your world."

He frowned. "But you would want to be with me if you could?"

"Well," she hesitated and the flush crept into her cheeks again. "We only spent one night together. That hardly makes a relationship. I don't even know you."

His heart ached as if someone had kicked him in the chest. He stared down at his syrup-smeared plate for a moment then looked back up at her. "But, Chrissy, I *know* you. I know we're meant to be together."

"We... We had a fantastic time together last night," she stammered. "Of course I'm in lust with you, but love... That's another thing altogether. I just couldn't say that so soon."

Gareth felt the food he'd eaten settle in his stomach like lead. His feeling for this woman was so strong, he'd been certain she felt it, too. He shrugged. "Never mind. We will not speak of it. Let's go now. I wish to see your city and some of the other things man has made." He pointed at a skyscraper in the distance. "There must be many stairs to get to the top of that building. I would like to climb them and see the view." He glanced at Chrissy and she looked relieved he'd dropped the subject.

"All right." She smiled. "I'm gonna show you some amazing things today."

Lila woke with a snort. Her eyes flew open and her mouth snapped shut. Her tongue was fuzzy from sleeping with her mouth wide open. From the sun pouring through the window, she guessed it was noon or later. She licked her dry lips then remembered her guest and rolled to her side to see if Zach was awake.

He lay sprawled on the makeshift pallet, but the cushions and covers had been knocked all over the place and he was half-on, half-off them. He slept on his back with one arm flung above his head, T-shirt riding up almost to his chest.

Lila got another good and uninterrupted view of his torso. It was damn fine.

The trail of light brown hair that led from his navel to the waistband of his jeans begged to be traced. Lila's fingers itched to do it then to keep right on going, unsnapping and unzipping his fly to find out if Zach had on the tighty-whiteys she imagined he wore.

She dragged her gaze away from the bulge in his crotch and up to his sleeping face.

Lush eyelashes swept across his pale cheeks. His straight nose jutted over a sweet, soft mouth, relaxed in repose.

Lila longed to kiss him awake and see the surprise register in his eyes when he opened them to find her hovering over him. She craved to plunge her hands into his silky, white-boy hair, to feel the sandy blond locks slip between her fingers. Her pussy grew wet from just thinking about it.

She sat up, shrugging the naughty thoughts from her mind and slipped out of bed. Stepping over Zach's prone body, she padded downstairs to the bathroom.

She was a little alarmed to find the rest of the house empty. Lila knew Taylor was at work, but had no idea where Chrissy had taken Gareth. Stupid girl hadn't even left a note. She started back upstairs to see if Zach was awake, only to find him descending to the first floor.

"Hey." He raised a hand in a morning welcome. "Slept like a baby last night."

"Me, too. I didn't think I'd be able to with everything going on." She gestured at the empty living room. "Unfortunately, Chrissy's taken off with our time traveler and you and I can't do any more work until the parts arrive, so I don't know exactly what to do."

Zach came down the last few steps. "We could eat brunch and take a walk to clear our heads. It's a beautiful, sunny afternoon."

Lila glanced at the bright sunshine pouring through the living room window. A walk in the park sounded wonderful. "Someone has to be here to sign for the package. We can't really leave."

"We'll track it online. Might not have even left the warehouse yet. We'll keep our walk short." Zach's eyes were guileless and pleading.

Lila was beginning to wonder if his geek image was an act and he wasn't a bit of a player underneath. He sure knew how to charm her into agreement. "All right. A short walk. You check the shipping. I'll make something to eat."

Zach bounded back upstairs like a Great Dane.

Lila smiled as she noticed he was wearing one black sock and one brown. The nerd thing was definitely for real.

A short meal and long discussion of fractals later, Lila and Zach left the house to walk in the nearby park.

"How's your dissertation coming along?" Lila looked up at the leaf-laced branches overhead and tried to ignore her crazy impulse to hold Zach's hand as they strolled.

"Don't remind me. I'm stalled. My workload is crazy this year. I'm teaching two of Professor Donnelly's classes and substituting for him in his other classes every time he's drunk, which is about every other day."

"Professors." Lila shook her head, smiling. "How I miss the academic life. Wish I could get a grant for my work and chuck the lab job."

"I can't wait to be finished with school, get into a research lab and start putting theory into practice like you have. The work you've done is...amazing."

"And dangerous." She stopped to look at a couple of kids feeding the ducks at the edge of the pond. "I was so set on using this technology to improve the world, I closed my eyes to the possible negatives. Besides the issue of interfering with time, there's also the possibility the government could find some way to misuse it."

Zach led the way to a bench facing the pond and they sat. "I thought of that, too, but didn't want to say anything. Maybe I'm paranoid from watching too many movies where the military fucks things up, but you've got to be careful who you share your discovery with."

"I know." Lila squinted against the sun glinting off the water. "I should probably destroy it after I send Gareth back." Her heart clenched as she thought of the countless wasted hours she'd devoted to her dream. "But, God, it hurts to let it go." Tears prickled her eyes and she was embarrassed to feel her lip trembling. The weight of Zach's arm slipped around her shoulders, warm and heavy, making her feel strangely secure.

"Don't do anything right away. Think about it for a while." He held her tight against his side, his body angled toward hers.

Lila looked up into Zach's eyes. She could see he wanted to kiss her.

He inclined his head, his left hand reaching up to cup the side of her face.

Lila leaned toward him, drawn as if by an invisible magnet. Then she suddenly realized what she was doing, pulled back and turned away.

Zach dropped his hand from her cheek and removed his arm from her shoulders. "Why not?" he said simply.

"I'm sorry. We're friends, but I'm not interested in you like that. You're not..."

"Not your type? Which part is the problem? Too skinny, too geeky, too white or all of the above?"

"No. It's not like that," she protested, although yesterday she would've answered yes to all of the above. "It's just I have a certain kind of guy I'm attracted to and—"

"I'm not it. Got it." Zach rose from the bench abruptly then extended a hand to help Lila to her feet.

"I'm sorry," she repeated as he drew her to her feet.

He shrugged. "Doesn't matter. I'm supposed to be here to help you, not hit on you." He stepped close to her, invading her personal space and looking deep into her eyes. "But don't think academic means sexless. I may not be chockfull of muscles like our friend Conan the Barbarian, but muscles don't make a man. And despite what you say, I think you're interested in me, too."

Lila opened her mouth to argue.

Zach bent his head and kissed her firmly, stopping her words. His lips were warm and yielding, but the kiss was hard and masterful.

She responded automatically, her mouth parting under his. She rested her hands against his chest and felt his heart beating strongly beneath her palms.

After kissing her for one long, breathless moment, he straightened and let her go without trying to take it further.

Her lips vibrated with energy and her body craved more contact. Her fingers clutched the fabric of his T-shirt, unwilling to let go.

"Still sure I'm not your type?" Zach's voice was low and seductive. He cocked an eyebrow at Lila then disengaged her grip on his shirt and turned away from her. Without a backward glance, he headed up the path. "We should probably get back in case that package arrives."

Chapter Five

Zach made a conscious effort to saunter casually along the walk. He couldn't hold back the grin that stretched his mouth, but since Lila was behind him, she couldn't see it. *Score one for the boy!* He'd left her shaken and breathless. Before he turned away, he saw it in her wide brown eyes and open mouth.

Zach didn't know what had given him the balls to just lay one on her like that, but it made him feel empowered. This must be what men like Gareth felt like all the time, never bumbling over words or tripping on their own feet, always in control of the situation. Zach felt as cool as James Bond.

Lila caught up with him and he wiped the smile off his face.

They walked silently, side by side back to her house.

It was a good thing they'd returned. The FedEx truck was about to pull away from the curb. Lila ran and flagged it down then signed for the package of crucial components.

Up in Lila's workroom, Zach began to second-guess the kiss and his cocky confidence oozed away. The silence between them remained awkward and strained, the kiss unacknowledged. Their encounter hung in the air, spoiling the easy banter they'd enjoyed before, making conversation stilted as they worked on the project.

"No, like this." Lila leaned over to demonstrate something.

Zach breathed in her perfumed skin and watched her slender brown hands move delicately over the reconstruction. "Okay."

She sat back in her seat, resuming her own task.

The house was as quiet as if it were the dead of night. Zach could hear small creaks and the hum of the refrigerator two floors down as he carefully soldered a component in place. He wished Chrissy and the barbarian would show up just to break the tension.

After twenty minutes in the torturous vacuum of silence, Lila exploded. She slapped her tiny screwdriver on the counter and turned to Zach. "Why'd you have to do that, dammit? Now things are all weird between us."

"Do what?" He played dumb for all of two seconds then sighed. "Look, I'm sorry. I thought that's what you wanted. Somebody more...assertive. A take-charge kinda guy."

"Did I say that? Did you ever hear me say that?" She rose, folding her arms over her chest. "Now our friendship's all screwed up 'cause there's *that* hanging over our heads."

Zach pushed away from the bench and stood to face her. "It was just a kiss, Lila. But if it got you this worked up then there must be something there—some spark between us."

She shook her head vigorously. "No. No, there isn't. We're science buddies. Internet pals. That's all. I told you, you're not my type."

"Bullshit! You kissed me back, and not the way science buddies do." He grabbed the back of his chair and sent it rolling across the floor. "What the hell do women want? All the nice guys get passed over for not being 'bad' enough? Fuck that, I don't want to be your nice, safe friend."

Zach crossed the space between them. Once more he leaned down and kissed Lila, and this time he wasn't polite about it. He encompassed her lips, tasting some kind of fruity lipgloss as he sucked their sweet fullness into his mouth. He cupped the back of her head with one hand and the side of her face with the other, holding her steady as he swept his tongue inside her mouth and showed her that nice guys could kiss, too.

She made a brief, high-pitched noise, either of surprise or pleasure, he wasn't sure which, but her hands slid up his back and curved around his shoulders, holding on tight.

Zach didn't know if he was going to get another chance like this so he kissed her for all he was worth, feeding at her lips as if she were his last meal on death row. His tongue delved into the heat of her mouth and curled around her tongue. He moved his hand from her neck to slide it slowly all the way down her spine to her waist. After a brief hesitation, he dropped down farther to cup her round ass in his hand.

Lila made another soft, little sound. This time it definitely qualified as a moan. She pressed her pelvis against his, rubbing against the bulge in his jeans.

Zach felt sparks of electricity shooting between them at the point of contact. He knew it wasn't possible, but his body told him the voltage was real. He groaned and thrust into her crotch.

She stumbled back against the workbench, lifting a leg to wrap it around his thigh.

He pulled back, chest rising and falling with his rapid breaths, and stared into Lila's dilated pupils for the space of five heartbeats, noting that she was gasping for breath, too. Then he swooped down to suck her bottom lip into his mouth once more. It was so full and rich and maulable.

"Mm. Mmph." Lila pressed against his chest and pulled her head away. "The project…"

A stab of disappointment speared through him. He knew this was too good to last.

"My ass is on it. We need to move to the bed."

"Oh. Yeah. Right," he stammered. With more strength than he knew he possessed, Zach hauled the girl up into his arms and carried her across the room. Her butt rested neatly in his hands, her legs girdled his waist and her arms clung around his neck like cables. Laying her carefully down on the bed, he knelt over her body.

She didn't let go of his neck, but pulled him right down on top of her. Both of her hands thrust into his hair, grabbing thick fistfuls of it as she mashed her lips against his.

His head spun at the sudden escalation of events, but he wasn't about to put on the brakes. Lying on top of Lila's soft, curvaceous body, he pressed her into the bed, rocking his hips and grinding his cock into her crotch.

Lila thrust up, embracing him with a thigh on either side of his hips.

Zach finally surrendered her lips, moving his mouth down to her jaw then her neck, scented with sandalwood. The aroma seemed part of her warm, brown skin, and he breathed in deeply, pressing his lips to the pounding pulse point just below her ear.

Laughing, she wiggled beneath him, twisting away from his tickling mouth.

He smiled and continued his journey down her neck to the sharp lines of her collarbones. He licked along the hard ridges then over the fleshy curve of her right shoulder. Lifting his head, he looked at her as he slipped the strap of her tank top down her shoulder.

She smiled her approval, watching him through heavy-lidded eyes.

Zach pulled down the strap on her left side, too, leaving her shoulders bare. He smoothed his hands over her shoulders then pulled her top down her chest, not quite baring her breasts.

Lila thrust her chest up and the top slid the rest of the way off her round breasts, revealing tightly puckered, mahogany nipples.

He descended on one breast like a hawk on a rabbit, engulfing the nipple and sucking it into his mouth greedily.

Grabbing his hand, she guided it to her other breast, which was lush and full as a tempting piece of fruit at the market that must be gently tested for ripeness.

Zach squeezed the tan globe, enjoying the weight of it filling his hand. Then he fondled her nipple, pinching it hard, then a little harder.

"Oh, baby, that feels so good," she murmured. "Just like that."

The growling purr of her voice was like velvet rubbing over his skin. The hairs on his arms and the back of his neck stood at attention. Lila was a talker. Wow! He was anxious to hear what else she might say if he moved down a little farther. He bunched the tank top under her breasts and continued kissing his way down her belly toward her jeans. Her flat stomach jumped and twitched under his trailing tongue. She tasted spicy and salty, a piquant flavor that made him want more.

He unbuttoned and unzipped the fly of her jeans, revealing wine-red, silky panties. They outlined her crotch in a neat vee edged with lace. Caressing the smooth material, he felt the swell of her mons and the springy mat of pubic hair beneath the underwear.

His dick had been growing steadily harder from the moment they'd kissed. Coming this close to the Holy Grail of her pussy was almost too much to bear. His cock vibrated in time to his heartbeats and he wondered if he might come from the sheer excitement of having Lila splayed half-nude before him. He bent his head and reverently kissed her crotch through those slippery underpants.

She moaned and lifted toward his mouth.

Zach blew a hot breath across the material then slipped his fingers under the elastic around her legs and teased his finger into the mysterious folds and steamy moisture of her pussy.

She raised her hips again. "Take them off." Her voice was breathless.

Zach didn't need more encouragement to strip the scrap of material and the denims down Lila's long, smooth legs and toss them aside. Again he blew over her crotch then breathed in her musky scent. He lowered his head and dipped his tongue into her wetness, lapping a stroke up her slit and over her labia.

She moaned louder. "Oh, yes."

He twirled his tongue around the hard nub of her clit, dancing in close but not touching it yet. He smiled as she squirmed and wiggled, and pressed his hands against her hips, pinning her to the bed.

"Please. Do it. Please," she whined.

God, he loved the sound of her begging. He continued to lick around her clit for a few more moments then relented and lapped across it.

"Ahhh," she breathed, thrusting her pussy toward his mouth despite his restraining hands. Her torso twisted on the bed, her back arching and her beautiful breasts jutting upward.

"Mm." Zach growled his appreciation of the sight and continued to devote himself to her pleasure, licking and sucking the tiny pink bud. His cock ached with the need to be inside her and he rubbed it against the bed.

Lila moaned and whimpered. "Yeah, oh yeah, yesssss," she hissed. "Uh-huh. Just. Like. That." She cried out and suddenly bucked hard against his hands and mouth.

Zach backed off and watched her go, writhing on the bed with abandon. It made him hotter than ever and absolutely desperate to climb on top of her and plunge inside.

Finally she collapsed with a long, drawn out exhalation, throwing her arms wide. "Whew! That was something." Her eyes opened and she looked at him with a big grin. "Baby, you got game."

Zach laughed and crawled up her body to lie between her spread legs, looking down into her deep brown eyes. "White boy can dance, too." He smiled and leaned down to kiss her lips. "Sorta," he added.

"Well, let's see how those hips move then," she teased, reaching down and pulling his shirt up his back.

He lifted one arm then the other so she could pull the T-shirt off him. It got caught on his head and Lila laughed as she tugged it free. She threw the shirt aside and ruffled his hair. "Cute. You're so damn cute." She reached down between their bodies and fumbled with the button on his jeans.

Zach's stomach jerked as her hands brushed his naked torso. He sucked in a breath through his teeth. This was really happening. His cock was going to be in her hand in a moment. He lifted himself higher so she could reach his fly and heard the tiny *snnnick* sound of his zipper going down then felt her warm hand delving inside his shorts and cupping his cock.

She stroked up and down once...twice...sending ripples of delight through him, then withdrew her hand and pushed his clothing down his hips.

Zach rolled to the side and shimmied out of them. Kicking off his shoes and whipping off his socks in record time he lay back on top of Lila. Beneath him, her body was as soft and yielding as a feather bed—a very warm, fleshy, womanly, feather bed.

Wrapping her arms around him, she caressed his back, smoothing her hands up and down his spine then over his shoulders.

He nestled his cock into the hard ridge of her pubic bone and rocked a little from side to side. Her thatch of hair tickled and aroused him.

Lila giggled. "Yeah. I guess you dance okay."

He grinned and continued to rub against her, stimulating her already sensitive clit with the slide of his cock.

Her eyes closed and she made a humming sound in her throat. "Want you inside me now," she whispered.

Hearing her ask for it sent Zach's pulse rocketing even faster and his cock throbbed with desire. "You have condoms?"

"Yeah." She squirmed out from underneath him and retrieved a packet from her nightstand, ripped it open and sheathed his shaft.

Zach positioned himself at her entrance, took a deep breath and pushed in. His dick was instantly enveloped in delicious heat. He slid into her depths with a satisfied groan. He didn't know if it was just her or because he hadn't been with a woman in a long time, but either way it felt like a perfect fit.

For a long moment he stayed inside simply enjoying the feel of Lila's body surrounding him, not only his cock but also her arms and legs wrapped around him. He buried his face in the side of her neck and breathed in the sandalwood scent again. Slowly he withdrew his full length then plunged back in again.

She stroked the back of his hair and murmured near his ear. "You feel so good inside me. You fill me up."

He'd never had sex with a talker before and found he loved the sound of her voice, her sexy murmurs spurring him on. Again he pulled out and thrust in, setting a slow and easy rhythm.

"Good. That's good. Now harder," she panted, clutching his ass and digging her fingers into his flesh.

He complied, grunting with every deep thrust.

Lila arched her hips each time. "Oh, baby..." Her words dissolved into whimpering moans and soft cries.

Zach lifted himself on his arms and looked down at her beautiful face, drawn into a parody of pain. Her eyebrows were knit together, her mouth open and gasping. Her magnificent breasts jiggled as he drove into her again and again.

His control slipped as his balls tightened and his cock pulsed in preparation for release. He groaned and rammed into her, plunging wildly.

His primal rutting only inflamed Lila. She cried out and arched beneath him as another orgasm blazed through her. "Aaaah!"

A moment later, his own orgasm crashed over him like a wave knocking him off his feet. Exquisite pleasure rolled through him and he cried out, too. "Jesus!" Closing his eyes, he rode the wave.

Afterward he collapsed on top of Lila, breathing heavily, stroking the tight curls of her thick hair and the smooth curve of her cheek. He kissed her shoulder, still in shock at the unexpected sex, but infinitely grateful for it.

"That was wonderful," she murmured, caressing her fingertips up and down his spine. She sighed and patted his rear. "But this doesn't get the time machine fixed."

"Mm." He mumbled into her shoulder. "Five more minutes of cuddling?"

"I guess five minutes couldn't hurt."

Ten minutes later, both of them were sound asleep.

Chapter Six

"So that's how the combustion engine works, as far as I understand it," Chrissy said as she unlocked the door and let them into the house. "You might want to ask Lila if you really want the facts."

"Amazing and so simple."

Gareth was fascinated by the twenty-first century and he was wearing her out with his questions. During the course of their outing, she'd learned she had no idea how refrigeration actually worked nor what made air flight possible. She had extemporized an explanation for airplanes, throwing around terms like "aerodynamics" as if she really understood them. Then she'd taken him to the Science and Industry Museum where he was enthralled by exhibits explaining everything from coal mining to microchips.

"Anyway, that's what I remember about engines from fifth-grade science class, but I'm sure it's a bit more complicated. Are you hungry again? I could whip up some dinner. Or maybe you'd rather check in with Lila and Zach first to see how the repairs to the time machine are going." She shook her head. "God, I feel so stupid saying 'time machine'. This whole thing is unbelievable."

"Why?" Gareth took off the jacket she'd bought him. "Why is your friend's machine more unbelievable than any of the other things you've shown me today?"

"Good point." Chrissy smiled. "Shall we go see Lila, then?"

He cocked his head to the side, looking at her. "Yes. But first..." He pulled her into his arms and kissed her.

"Mm." She leaned into his big, strong body and yielded to his searching mouth.

"Maybe..." Gareth moved his lips to her neck and nibbled up and down her throat. "We could wait to talk to Lila..." He dropped his head to lick along her collarbone. "Until later."

Chrissy tilted her head back and her eyes drifted closed. "Waiting is good. Whoa!"

Gareth swooped her up and carried her toward the stairs.

She flung her arms around his neck and held on, feeling like a maiden in a fairytale being carried off by a knight...or an invading barbarian.

"I've wanted to take you all day." His voice was hoarse and hungry.

Pressed tightly against his chest, Chrissy could feel the vibrations and a thrill shot up her spine at his words, *take you.* It sounded so primitive and exciting. She'd been having plenty of fantasies of taking and having throughout the day herself. Leaning in, she kissed the side of his neck just under the line of his beard. It was rough. He needed another shave. She imagined that stubble brushing her breasts and the insides of her thighs and shivered.

The part of her that wasn't lust-addled realized Lila had probably been waiting for them to come home and might be furious. As Gareth carried her past the steps to the third floor, Chrissy listened, but there was only silence upstairs. Lila and Zach were probably so deeply immersed in their project they'd totally tuned out the world. Scientist types were like that. Big-brained geeks.

Gareth turned the handle of Chrissy's bedroom door then kicked it open. He carried her across the threshold like a bridegroom and laid her on the bed.

She looked up at him as he removed his translating device and his clothes. Chrissy took out her own translator and laid it aside. There was something exotic and thrilling about having sex with a foreigner. The words of Gareth's guttural language, which at first had sounded harsh and rough to her ears, now poured over her like water.

"H'rath ni craught, Chrissy. Tu vueltan?"

"Oh, yes," she breathed, lifting her arms so he could peel off her shirt. "Definitely. I'd love to do whatever you said." Chrissy lifted her hips and Gareth tugged off her jeans. "But you'll go down on me first, right? 'Cause, wow, you've got some skills."

"Valizcro janus mi drogan." Gareth towered over her, caressing the long, hard length of his shaft as he gazed at her.

"You're saying I make you hard?" She scooted to the edge of the bed and took him in hand, rubbing his ridged member lightly. "You make me hard, too. My pussy is aching for you."

"Poissee," Gareth repeated, fondling her hair. "Amara tu poissee."

"And I love that you love my pussy." Chrissy opened her mouth and sucked his cock into her mouth. Her lips stretched to encircle the huge member. She slid as much of it as she could deep into her throat and rubbed her hand up and down the rest of the thick shaft.

Gareth groaned. His eyes drifted closed.

She relished the taste and texture of his satiny cock in her mouth. She could get used to this—to him, so easily. A sharp stab of realization hit her that it was going to be very hard to let Gareth go when it was time. She tightened her grip and stroked him harder, determined to remember every moment of their brief time together.

Taylor came home just before dusk, tossing her purse and keys on the table in the front hall and leaning against the door. Even with her sensible white shoes, her feet hurt like a bitch. It had been a long, exhausting day in PT. Mrs. Van Allen was whiny and tearful, Mr. Abernathy growly and gruff and little Sarah Vosters pissy and pouty. Yet throughout the parade of miserable patients, Taylor must maintain her sweet disposition, when everybody who knew her knew that she didn't *have* a naturally sweet disposition.

She wanted to snap at each one of the patients that they should be glad they were alive. They should bite the bullet, do the exercises and embrace the amazing days they were lucky to have. But, she'd long ago learned that most people didn't look at the positive. Especially not when they were uncomfortable, their bodies racked with pain.

The front hall and living room beyond were dark. "Anybody home?" She walked upstairs and got her answer as she passed Chrissy's door.

Gareth sounded like a freight train o' love, grunting and puffing rhythmically. Chrissy whimpered like a lovestruck puppy. "Oh, oh, ohhhh."

Taylor's nipples hardened at the arousing noises. Her pussy clenched and grew wet. "God, I need a date," she murmured to herself. She walked past Chrissy's closed door toward her own room then decided to go up and see Lila first to find out how the time machine project was coming along.

Taylor climbed the stairs and entered Lila's laboratory at the top of the house. It was actually a pretty cool space and she would've loved to have it for herself. The windows looked out over several blocks in every direction. The open floor and slanted eaves gave it a cozy, old-fashioned feeling as did Lila's vintage bedroom suite.

Taylor remembered the hot, hellacious day they'd dragged the heavy pieces of the bed up the two flights of stairs as she looked toward the bed—the bed on which Lila and a sandy-blond guy sprawled naked, their limbs tangled together, coffee brown and pale cream.

Holy shit, that must be MathMan. Taylor's eyes popped open at the unexpected erotic sight. "Damn, everybody's getting some but me!" Lila's eyes flew open, too. She sat up, throwing MathMan's arm off of her and tugging the sheet up to cover them both. "Taylor! Get out!"

"Sorry." She backed through the door. "I thought you'd be busy fixing the machine, but obviously you were gettin' busy a different way." She burst into giggles and waved hello at the tousle-haired MathMan, who sat up beside Lila.

He blinked and lifted a hand in acknowledgement.

"Out!" Lila threw a pillow that just missed Taylor's head.

She turned and left, laughing all the way back downstairs.

But by the time she'd reached her bedroom, kicked off her shoes and taken off her uniform, the humor in the situation had sort of drained away. She threw herself across her bed in her bra and underpants, lying on her back, staring up at the ceiling. *Sex above her, sex beside her and the buxom blonde in the house the only one not getting laid. Something was wrong with this picture.*

Taylor sighed and reached for the vibrator in her nightstand drawer. As she flipped it on and the quiet buzzing sound set her pussy on automatic alert, she decided she'd call Steve tonight, the guy her co-workers had been trying to hook her up with for weeks. "Steve, you may hit the jackpot on the first date," she said as she peeled off her thong and brought the tip of the vibrator to her clit.

"I can't believe how late it is. How could we have slept so long?" Lila crawled over Zach to get out of bed and began picking up discarded clothing from the floor.

He watched her. "It's okay. We'll work on it again now."

"It was irresponsible." She kept her eyes focused on her task. She didn't want to see him sitting in her bed with his flyaway hair and puppydog gaze. She hadn't meant to get involved with him and now she was afraid she'd see all sorts of expectations in his clear, green eyes. "Damn!" She straightened, her thong dangling from one hand. "What was I thinking? I've got the future of time travel in my hands, not to mention the fate of one displaced warrior. Fucking my...cyber-buddy and sleeping the afternoon away is not prudent at this juncture."

Zach slid out of bed, picked up his jeans and boxers and put them on.

Boxers, not tighty-whiteys, she registered.

"Calm down. We'll get right to work." His voice was reassuring, and maybe slightly hurt at her casual dismissal of their tryst.

Lila didn't know why she was so resistant to Zach. He was sweet, generous, shared her interests and intellect, and had just proved he was dynamite in the sack. Why was she shutting him out and giving him that "I made a mistake" vibe?

Once dressed, Lila felt a little less vulnerable. "Thank you." She forced herself to make eye contact with him. "It was very nice...I mean, good. It was great." She stumbled over the compliment.

Zach's eyes scanned hers for a moment as if looking for something then he nodded his head once. "My pleasure. Thank you, too." He crossed to the table and resumed the task he'd been working on. His rigid back telegraphed his disappointment.

She sighed. Instead of relieving the tension between them, having sex had made it worse. It was going to be a long night working together.

Chrissy woke with a start and looked up to find Gareth watching her.

He smiled and brushed a tendril of hair from her cheek. "Amara, Chrissy," he murmured. He bit his bottom lip then said haltingly and with the appropriate pointing gestures, "You. Go. Me."

She swallowed. She was half-asleep and not ready to have this discussion again. "No. I can't. I belong here. I'm sorry."

Gareth understood her negative tone. He frowned and muttered something unintelligible.

Anxious to escape the impossible conversation, Chrissy swung her legs out of bed. "Let's go to the kitchen and make some dinner for everybody." She dressed and slipped the translator back into her ear then turned to face him.

Gareth stood, clothed, by the side of the bed, holding her stuffed, plush rabbit which she'd owned since she was five. He fondled one of the floppy ears, long since worn free of any plush, then dropped the toy on the bed. He looked at her. "I could stay here."

Her heart jolted in her chest. She couldn't deny the idea had crossed her mind, but it was impossible—wasn't it? "If you didn't live out the life you were meant to live, the whole course of the world might change." Even as she parroted the theory that had been drilled into her in *Back to the Future* 101, Chrissy thought the idea seemed ridiculous. Butterfly wings and hurricanes be damned. Surely the loss of one man in the long course of history wouldn't make that big of a difference.

"Maybe *this* is the life I'm supposed to live," Gareth said, striding around the end of the bed and taking her hands. "Right here. With you."

Her pulse raced and a red flag went up in Chrissy's head. She'd never thought of herself as commitment-phobic, but they'd only met yesterday and his assertion they should be together for life was alarming.

"I don't know." She couldn't meet his intense eyes. "Um... Let's take this a little slower, okay? I'll think about what you said, trust me I will, but for now let's go downstairs and eat." As if to punctuate her words, her stomach rumbled loudly.

Gareth smiled slightly and nodded. "All right. My mother always said not to make important decisions on an empty stomach."

"Mine, too! Hundreds of years later and mothers are still saying that." She laughed, slipped her arms around Gareth's waist and rested her head on his huge, hard chest.

His hand rubbed up and down her back. "I will not speak of it again, Chrissy, but know that I am ready to stay here if you tell me you want me to."

She nodded against his chest. It felt so good and right to be in his arms, she wondered why she had any doubts about it at all.

Taylor swayed back and forth with her arms lifted over her head, grinding her hips to the thumping bass. Electronic dance music pulsed and lights strobed in the dark club. In her sequined bra and black miniskirt, she was in her element dancing and drinking the night away. She whirled to face her dance partner. Unfortunately, he wasn't part of her element.

Despite her co-workers' insistence that Steve was "just her type", he absolutely wasn't. Tall, dark and handsome, check, but his personality was Shallow Hal without the charm. How had anyone thought she would hit it off with such a jackass? It made Taylor feel they didn't know her at all.

But as long as she kept on dancing, she wouldn't have to talk to him, so Taylor turned her back to Steve and began gyrating to the beat.

It had been a crazy evening from the beginning. First she had to sit at the dinner table with the two sets of lovers—Gareth and Chrissy sneaking surreptitious glances at one another the whole meal, Lila and Zach hardly making eye contact at all. The sexual tension in the air was so thick you could spread butter on it, making Taylor feel like an old-maid chaperone.

Arranging a date with Steve had taken only a quick phone call. After dinner, she'd enjoyed a long bubble bath and dressing up for clubbing. It took her almost a half-hour just to apply her make-up. When she opened the door and saw Steve, her heart fluttered with anticipation. He was model beautiful with perfect white teeth, dark eyes and artistically tousled hair. His shirt strained over his chest and his biceps bulged.

"Hell-o!" Taylor favored him with a brilliant smile. "I should have called *you* a long time ago." She scanned his body lasciviously, thinking this evening might be quite pleasant.

Then Steve began to speak and the myth was busted. The man was an idiot, boring on the way to the restaurant, self-involved over drinks, obnoxious in the car ride to the club, and a jerk every time he spoke over the driving dance music. He was the epitome of a smarmy player.

As Taylor shimmied against his hard body on the dance floor, she thought maybe she could ignore his personality and just enjoy a good lay. He certainly felt good pressing against her and writhing in time with her movements. If they were that in sync in the bedroom, the evening didn't have to be a total loss.

But when they finally left the club after one o'clock and began making out in his car, Steve went and opened his mouth again. "Baby, do you have a map, 'cause I keep getting lost in your eyes. Your place or mine?"

"Ah, nuh-uh." Taylor shook her head and pushed him away from her neck. "Home, please." Yes, she'd wanted mindless sex, but not this mindless.

"Aw, come on. Jamie said—"

"What did Jamie say?" Taylor knew her co-workers thought she was a little slutty—all right a lot slutty—and maybe they were right, but knowing that's all they perceived her as was painful. "That I'd put out?"

"Well..." Steve trailed off.

"Are you taking me home or am I catching a taxi?" She shouldn't have asked. Her opinion of Steve was confirmed when she found herself hailing a cab in the middle of the night on a dark, empty street.

Tumbling into bed later, Taylor, who'd always lived her life like a party, had a rare moment of introspection. *I'm tired of one-nighters and men who are as shallow as I am.*

She thought about Lila and Chrissy's sudden bond with their new men. Observing the couples, she'd sensed a palpable force between each set of lovers. She'd never really believed in love at first sight, but witnessing the almost cosmic connection was starting to make her a believer.

Where's my connection? Where's my other half? Taylor rolled over and buried her face in her pillow. She needed a new kind of man, nothing like the self-involved assholes she'd been hooking up with. Maybe someday in the future guys wouldn't be so oblivious about what women wanted. Maybe in the future men would be attentive, sensitive, and in tune with a woman's needs.

Someday the whole dating thing had to get better. Someday men had to improve. Taylor's eyes widened and she sat up in bed. Some day didn't have to be so far away.

Chapter Seven

Gareth embraced Chrissy one last time, then she practically shoved him away. "I really have to go. I'm gonna be late and I'll miss my bus. Relax. Eat whatever you can find that's edible in the kitchen, and ask Lila if you need help with something. I'll be back from work in about eight hours."

He watched her firm ass sway beneath her skirt as she walked down the sidewalk. A half block away, she turned and waved. He was ashamed at how abandoned he felt seeing her disappear around the corner, like a small boy left behind by his mother. It was ridiculous.

Gareth went back inside the house and to the kitchen, where he filled a glass with water and drank it down. His throat was dry and scratchy and the headache he'd woken up with that morning was getting worse. Filling the glass, he drank again then watched the water pour down the drain for a moment, thinking about the endless trips to the village well, the nearest stream or rainwater barrel the women in his village had to take every day as they cleaned and cooked. This new world was truly astounding, yet the people in it showed no appreciation for its wonders.

Wandering into the living room, he sat on the soft, fabric-covered chair, which molded comfortably to his body. The brilliant blue eyes of a beautiful blonde woman on the cover of Taylor's magazine caught his attention. He picked up the glossy booklet and flipped through the pages. They were full of beautiful women of all shapes, sizes and skin colors, many of them scantily clad and most with lips and eyes painted unnatural colors. Gareth gazed at the pretty women until his cock began to harden. He was surprised it had the energy left to rise after the exercise Chrissy had put it through last night.

He started to close the magazine then caught a whiff of something that smelled like wood smoke and sage. Bending his head toward the book, he sniffed until he found the page that smelled. There was a picture of a smooth-shaven young man with a hairless chest, a beautiful woman swooning at his feet and a glass bottle of amber colored liquid—a magic potion the young man used to make the woman love him. Gareth leaned down and inhaled near the folded edge of the paper where the scent was strongest. When he opened the flap, the woodsy smell was even stronger. Suddenly he knew what he needed to do.

Chrissy didn't love him as strongly as he loved her. When he'd talked about staying in this world, her eyes had not lit up nor had she smiled. It was clear she loved having sex with him, but didn't really love *him*. If he drank some of this potion, perhaps he could change that.

He stared at the amber bottle of liquid and wondered where he might purchase it and how he could get some modern day coins with which to buy it. The matter was very complicated.

Maybe there was enough potion on the page to cause the desired effect. Bringing the paper to his mouth, he licked it from bottom to top. Gareth scowled at the vile taste and closed the magazine. What a stupid idea. He couldn't force Chrissy to love him more than she did and he didn't want her if he could only win her that way. Besides, one lick of the magic potion probably wouldn't be effective.

Tossing the magazine aside, he pondered what to do next. He felt so useless in this time and place. He'd always had a purpose in his life and now had none but to sit and wait for his lover to return and for the dark witch to send him home.

Gareth gazed at the silent picture box across the room. Maybe it could offer a few hours of diversion while he waited. He picked up the small black device that had power over the box and pushed several buttons, but nothing happened. "Zahrgratz!" he cursed, shaking the device.

"Hey, man. Can I help you with that?" Lila's lover stood in the doorway of the living room. When Gareth looked up, the man raised his hands to show he wasn't armed. "Don't attack me again, okay?"

The man wore one of the translators, so Gareth spoke to him. "I'm sorry. I thought you had broken into the house. I didn't know you belonged with Lila."

"Belonged?" The man gave a sharp laugh as he walked into the room. "I wish. Sometimes it's hard to tell what women want, you know? What the hell they expect from a guy. My name's Zach, by the way." He held out his hand.

Gareth shook it. "Gareth."

"Let me show you how this works." Zach crouched beside the chair and demonstrated how to use the controller to turn the picture box on and change the picture inside.

Gareth began to turn the channel again and again. The effect of colorful images and movement was hypnotic. He was mesmerized for several moments until Zach's laughter broke his concentration.

"Welcome to the twenty-first century. Channel surfing is one of the prime pastimes of the American male."

Gareth frowned, not getting the joke.

"Never mind. Enjoy. I've got to get back upstairs and be useful." Zach clapped him on the shoulder and left the room.

For a while Gareth stared at the flashing images on the box. With no sun to measure the passing of the day, he wasn't sure how long he watched, but when he broke from his trance-like state, the ache behind his eyes thudded with each heartbeat. That's when Gareth realized the magic box was putting some sort of evil spell on him.

He felt much worse than he had earlier. His temples pounded and his throat was so swollen he could hardly swallow his own saliva.

He turned the pictures off and got up. Blood rushed from his head and he felt dizzy. Some fresh air would help clear his head. In the kitchen, he drank another glass of water then went outside. Instantly he felt better as he breathed in a deep draught of cool air and his head cleared a little.

After walking the paths in the park for a while and watching the children playing, he thought he'd like to see more of the city...maybe even surprise Chrissy at her work.

Gareth headed down the sidewalk in the direction she had gone to catch her bus.

It was after one o'clock when the time machine was re-assembled. Lila stepped back and examined the control panel and monitor. She went through a mental checklist of everything they'd repaired, looked at the schematic and back at her machine, then turned to Zach. "That should be it."

"Are you sure the modification I made will work?"

"There's only one way to find out."

"And what if it isn't right? What if we send Gareth into limbo and can't get him back? Or send him to the wrong point in time? Or fry him?" Zach's eyes were wide and worried. "Jesus. This is scary."

Lila nodded, staring at the invention she almost wished she hadn't created. "I know. Maybe we should transport an inanimate object first and see how that works."

"After we eat," Zach said. "I'm starving."

Lila suddenly remembered Gareth. "Shoot, Gareth must be, too. I haven't checked on him all morning."

"I went down earlier and he was watching TV. I'm sure he's fine."

But when they went downstairs, the living room was silent, the television turned off and Gareth was nowhere in sight.

Her stomach flipped.

"I'll check the bathroom." Zach headed for the stairs.

She did a quick sweep of the downstairs, calling Gareth's name, then went upstairs.

Zach met her in the hall, shaking his head. "Not up here."

Lila tapped at Taylor's door then knocked...then pounded, before finally opening the door and walking in. Her roommate was a small lump underneath the covers. Not even her head showed above the blankets. She twitched the covers back. "Wake up. Have you seen Gareth?"

Taylor opened one mascara-smudged eye. "What?" she whimpered. "Don't talk so loud."

"Gareth. Have you seen him?"

"Do I look like I've seen him?" She sat up, yawning and running a hand through her tangled blonde curls. "What'd he do, wander off again? God, we need a lo-jack on that guy."

"Get up and get dressed. We have to find him. He could be anywhere in the city by now." Lila's heart raced. She felt like she'd lost her child in a shopping mall. "Anything could have happened to him."

"Want me to call Chrissy?" Taylor swung her legs out of bed, noticed Zach standing in the doorway and pulled the sheet up to cover her nudity.

"No!" Lila decided she felt more like the babysitter who'd lost her employer's kid in the mall. "Not yet. There's no need to worry Chrissy about it. We'll find him."

Taylor yawned, winced and rubbed her eyes. "Well, he was in the park last time. I'd start there."

"While we look, you should call hospitals and the police in case he's been picked up," Zach suggested.

"Police? Oh my God," Lila groaned.

Lila and Zach each wore a translator so either one of them could communicate with Gareth if they found him. She wished she'd made more of the useful devices. They walked through the park in opposite directions calling for Gareth as if he were a lost dog, but by the time they met up again on the far side of the park, neither had found him.

She was almost in tears and had a strong urge to fling herself into Zach's warm embrace for comforting. "What are we going to do? He could be anywhere!"

He rubbed a hand up and down her arm. "He's not a child. I'm sure he can find his way back home again."

"But what if he got mugged or something?"

"Then he probably killed the mugger and scalped him."

Lila frowned.

"Sorry. Let's go back and see if Taylor found out anything. If he got hit by a car or hurt in some way, he'd be at the hospital, right? And if he got into trouble, he'd be at a police station. But probably he's simply out sightseeing."

Zach's reasonable tone made her feel better. She slipped her hand in his and squeezed it. "I haven't thanked you enough for helping me through this whole crisis. When I called you, you came, just like that. I can't tell you how grateful I've been for your...calmness through everything."

He shrugged. "That's what friends do, come when they're called." He stopped walking and looked down into Lila's eyes, a frown furrowing his brow. "I hope at least we're still friends—even if you don't want to be anything more."

Lila was saved from having to answer when her cell phone rang.

"Found him," Taylor said. "He's at Precinct Twenty-three charged with armed robbery, resisting arrest and, get this, public nudity. You'd better get over there fast."

"Oh my God," Lila groaned. "How are we going to get Gareth out of this with no ID or visa? He might be deported as an illegal alien. Shit!"

"So I shouldn't call Chrissy yet?"

"No!"

"All right. Calm down," Taylor said. "Okay, when you go to the police, Gareth is your cousin. Or maybe Zach's cousin would work better. I told the cops he was developmentally disabled and visiting from Bulgaria and he'd wandered off."

"Good cover." Lila was impressed. "If Chrissy calls, just tell her the machine is fixed. Zach and I've decided to test run it and if that works, we'll send Gareth home."

They arrived at the bustling precinct to find Gareth handcuffed and sitting on a chair in front of one of the desks as an officer typed up a report. He was in profile to Lila and didn't see her arrival. He looked pale and sullen.

She went to the officer at the front desk. "Hello, sir. I'm here for," she pointed, "that man over there."

"He's my cousin," Zach put in.

"From Bulgaria."

"He's mentally impaired. I was supposed to be looking after him, but I left him alone for a few minutes and he wandered off," Zach explained.

"Can we please just take him home?" Lila asked.

The desk sergeant shook his head. "It's too late for that. There's already paperwork."

At the same moment, Gareth glanced up and caught sight of them. He rose, pointing at them and jabbering at the arresting officer.

"Sit down!" The cop stood and held up his hands, gesturing Gareth back into his seat.

Lila could see things escalating quickly out of control. She had visions of Gareth getting gunned down right in the middle of the station. He was trying to explain his connection to Lila and Zach, but the policeman only saw a huge man, who'd already resisted arrest, looming over his desk.

"Wait! It's okay. Gareth, sit down!" She turned to the duty officer. "Please, can we just go over there and explain things?"

The man at the front desk glanced at the other officer, who nodded and beckoned them toward him.

Zach touched Lila's arm and whispered, "Let me talk. Gareth's my 'cousin'."

She nodded. It wouldn't do for them to give conflicting stories.

"Hello, sir. I'm sorry about all of this." Zach shook the cop's hand. "My name's Zach Meyer. This is my...girlfriend, Lila, and Gareth's my cousin. I can explain everything."

"Officer John McManus," the cop introduced himself. He was a short, stocky man with a gray crew cut and a rumpled blue uniform. "Your cousin is in pretty serious trouble here. Why don't we go back to one of the interview rooms and talk?"

Lila wondered if she should request a lawyer first, but prayed they could extricate Gareth before things got that serious.

"This band of warriors captured me and brought me to their stronghold. I'm sorry," Gareth said to Lila as McManus escorted them through the station. "You mustn't pay their ransom. I'll find a way to get free." He broke off in a fit of coughing.

"No," Lila hissed. "Just keep quiet and don't do anything. Let Zach talk."

McManus looked at Lila and Gareth sharply. He led the trio to a small room with a table and several folding chairs. After they were seated, he spoke to Zach. "What's your cousin's name?"

"Gareth...Schmidt." There was barely a pause while Zach thought up a last name. "Like I told the guy at the front desk, he's from a distant branch of our family in Bulgaria. He and my aunt are visiting for a month. Gareth is mentally impaired. I thought he was watching television in the living room and when I went to check on him, he was gone."

"Did you bring his passport with you?"

"Um, no. My aunt has it and she's on a... My mother took her on a sight-seeing trip today and they don't have a cell, so I can't contact her."

Lila listened, fascinated as Zach spun out the tale. His clear eyes and open face were so guileless she could almost believe him herself.

"What exactly has Gareth done, sir?"

"He threatened a store clerk at knife-point and stole a..." McManus glanced down at the report as if he couldn't quite believe the words he'd written. "Bottle of men's cologne. The clerk called 911. My partner and I spotted a man matching the clerk's description only a block away from the shop, urinating in an alley. When we attempted to arrest him, he resisted. I was forced to use a Taser in order to remove the knife from his possession and handcuff him."

Lila sucked in her breath. This was very bad. There was no way the cops were going to release Gareth without seeing his visa and verifying Zach's story first. Even with the extenuating circumstance of mental health issues, Gareth would face charges.

"Officer," Zach said. "May I talk to my cousin a moment? He's usually very harmless. I'm sure he was simply frightened. If you'll give me a chance to get his side of the story..."

McManus nodded.

Zach turned to Gareth. "Can you tell me what happened?"

Bonnie Dee

Gareth's hands in the metal cuffs clenched against the table surface. "Who are these people? What do they want?"

"You stole something. These men are...law officers. Understand?"

"The potion?" Gareth frowned. "I tried to give the man my knife in exchange for the potion since I didn't have money, but he didn't want it. He told me to take it and go."

"You were trying to trade with him?"

"Yes. And then this one," he nodded toward McManus, "and his cohort, set upon me as I was relieving myself."

Zach turned to McManus. "My cousin wanted the cologne as a gift for his grandfather in Bulgaria. He was trying to trade his dagger for it. Gareth doesn't understand about money. In his village everyone knows about his disability and they, uh, let him trade for little things he wants."

The cop frowned at the unlikely story. "He understands English but doesn't speak it?"

"Yes." Zach said. "Look, if he returns the cologne and apologizes to the shopkeeper, do you think the man would drop charges?"

Officer McManus sighed and massaged his temples. Clearly he didn't want to be involved with a delicate case involving a mentally impaired foreigner. The use of the Taser on a handicapped man could be construed as police brutality and an international incident with global news

136

coverage might mushroom from a simple misunderstanding. "Sit tight a moment. I'll be right back." McManus rose and left the room.

Immediately Zach turned to Gareth. "What's this about a potion? What were you trying to do?"

Gareth blushed and looked down at his manacled hands. "I know it was wrong. But when I saw the same potion from the magazine, I thought it was a sign I should try it after all."

"Try what? What the hell are you talking about?" Lila demanded.

"The love potion. In the picture, the young man took it and his woman fell in love with him." He sighed. "I know I must let Chrissy decide on her own, but she has bewitched me."

"I get it, man." Zach nodded. "Any lengths sometimes, right? But, seriously, you didn't drink any of that stuff did you? It's not really a love potion. It's to make you smell good and you could get sick if you swallowed it."

Gareth shook his head.

"'Cause you look kinda sick to me," Zach insisted.

Lila glanced at Gareth's pale, sweating face and realized he was right. Gareth looked terrible. She leaned over and put a hand on his forehead. It was hot. "My God, you're right. He has a fever."

"That's not good. He's got no immunity to all the diseases in this century."

Lila's mind flashed on whole tribes of Native Americans wiped out by smallpox brought by European settlers. "Crap, we should get him to the hospital."

The door opened and McManus re-entered the room with a file folder in one hand. He crossed to the chair and sat again. "All right. I talked to Mr. Pandanji and explained the unusual situation. He'll drop the charges."

Lila exhaled loudly. "Oh, thank you, Officer."

"Under the circumstances I won't file any paperwork. Just keep a better eye on your cousin from now on," the police officer reprimanded. "You should probably keep knives away from him."

"Definitely," Zach said. "My dad has an antique collection of daggers on display and he must have—"

"Thank you so much, sir," Lila interrupted, accepting the confiscated weapon in its neat Ziploc bag from the cop.

Officer McManus ushered them out the door. Lila was astounded Zach had managed to extricate Gareth from his predicament without even having to show identification or give an address.

"Do you think he'll check into this further?" Lila asked as they walked toward Zach's car parked farther up the street.

"Nuh-uh." Zach shook his head. "That cop's anxious to sweep it under the rug. Nothing will come of it."

Gareth coughed and rubbed his wrists where the handcuffs had been. "I don't understand any of this."

"The shopkeeper thought you were threatening him with the knife. He reported the, uh, potion stolen so those policemen arrested you," Lila explained.

Understanding dawned in his eyes. "*Oh*, the magician thought I was robbing him."

"Yes." Lila handed the dagger back to Gareth and he slipped it up his sleeve. She'd almost forgotten how dangerous he could be. He was trained to fight and kill. Maybe she should've held on to all his weapons until they were ready to send him back.

Lila's cell phone rang. It was Taylor again. "So, what happened? Did you get him out?"

"Zach did. It was amazing. He was such a good liar, I almost believed the story."

Zach smiled and delivered a bow before unlocking his car.

"Anyway, we're bringing Cousin Gareth home." She hung up then checked Gareth's temperature with her hand again. "You're burning up. We'll get you some cold medicine." Lila opened the passenger door for him to get into the car.

He stood there staring at the vehicle for a second before climbing inside. Lila showed him how to fasten the seatbelt and reassured him when she noticed his nervous expression. "I forgot this is your first car ride. Don't worry. It's perfectly safe."

"I'll drive slow," Zach added, as he started the car.

She got in the back seat. "Please stop by the pharmacy on the way. I don't want to send Gareth back through time with an illness. We may have to keep him around a few more days until he gets better."

Lila thought Chrissy would be happy about the delay since she didn't seem to be in any hurry to have their time traveling guest go home.

Chapter Eight

Chrissy nodded as she listened to the loan applicant explain her financial situation in excruciating detail. She already knew she'd have to refuse the woman's loan. It was the worst part of her job and today it seemed more depressing than usual since all she could think about was the fact she didn't want to let Gareth go.

On the other hand, she didn't necessarily want him to stay forever with all that entailed. She'd only known him for two days and wasn't ready for instant commitment.

"Yes, Ms. Parkinson, your credit report *is* very good," she assured the woman, "but it isn't enough. I'm sorry, but the bank has denied your loan."

Ms. Parkinson was one of the good ones. Although distressed, she took the news with grace, gathered her paperwork and left with a handshake. Chrissy feared the day one of her rejected applicants would come back into the bank with a semi-automatic.

Stretching, she dropped her high heels off her feet and rubbed them together beneath her desk then rotated her chair to and fro. She stared at the clock, willing the last twenty minutes of work to pass, feeling giddy as a young girl counting the minutes until she secretly meets her summer fling. Soon she'd see Gareth again, feel his hands caress her skin and his mouth covering hers. She'd hear his deep rumbling voice sending tingles through her body. Oh, no, she wasn't addicted to him. No way.

An hour later she finally walked through the front door of the house. She was glad today was Taylor's day off work because it meant a home-cooked meal. The scent of spicy tomato sauce wafted from the kitchen.

"Hey," Chrissy called, hanging her jacket and dumping her keys on the table.

Taylor came out from the kitchen. "Hi. Your boyfriend's sick."

"What?" Her heart jumped.

"He's got a fever. We gave him cold medicine, but I don't think it's working. Lila and MathMan are upstairs doing a trial run with the time machine, sending an apple back to 1962 to make sure it doesn't blow up before they use the machine on Gareth." She wiped her hands on the dishtowel she was holding and her eyes slid away from Chrissy's. "Anyway, Lila won't send Gareth back until he's well. You might want to go check on him."

Chrissy felt there was more Taylor wasn't saying. "What else happened today?"

"Nothing really. It turned out to be no big deal after all."

"What?" Chrissy demanded sharply.

"Well, your barbarian wandered off and got himself arrested, but Zach got the cops to let him go."

142

"What!?"

Taylor explained briefly how Gareth had gotten in and out of trouble.

"Oh my God, wasn't anybody watching him? How could you guys let this happen?"

"Hey, he's not two, and he's not mentally impaired, although that made a great cover story. How would we know he'd take it into his head to go find you? It won't matter soon anyway. Gareth will be back where he belongs, right? And nobody any the worse for it." She lifted an eyebrow, giving Chrissy a significant look.

"What?" Chrissy was really getting tired of hearing herself say it.

"How long have we known each other?" Taylor folded her arms and gazed at her with uncompromising blue eyes. "Three years, four? I've seen you date guys but I've never seen you like this before."

"Meaning?" She varied her vocabulary.

Taylor leaned against the frame in the kitchen doorway. "You're in love, girlfriend. Admit it. You're in love with that big brute of a barbarian."

It was Chrissy's turn to let her eyes slide away like a schoolgirl caught cheating. She shrugged. "I like him. But it doesn't matter how I feel. I can't live in his world and he can't stay here." She turned and started for the stairs.

Her bedroom was dark, the shades drawn. Only a small nightlight illuminated the large lump lying on her bed. As Chrissy approached Gareth, he moaned quietly and rolled onto his back. The orange glow of the nightlight shone across his face, reflecting off a sheen of sweat.

She rested a hand on his hot forehead.

His eyes flickered open and he looked up at her. "Chrissy. Te granziata." His voice was harsh and rasping.

"This is not good," she murmured as she located the translator on her bedside table and inserted it in her ear. "You're really sick. I think I should take you to the emergency room."

"What is 'emergency room'?" he croaked hoarsely.

"A healing place." She sat on the bed and straightened the covers over him. "The medicine Lila gave you isn't working. You may have an infection and should be on an antibiotic."

Gareth breathed in deeply then started coughing.

Chrissy put her hand on his chest, feeling his breath rattling in and out. "God, this is really bad. I'm going to borrow Taylor's car and take you to a doctor." She knew the homeless could receive treatment, no questions asked, at the Rose Street Clinic. Rising, she pulled the covers off Gareth and helped him to sit.

His torso glistened with sweat like a wrestler oiled for a match.

Chrissy was ashamed that despite the circumstance of his fevered illness his gleaming muscles turned her on. She helped him into his shirt then knelt and put on his socks and shoes. He touched the crown of her head and she looked up at him.

"I love you," he whispered. "If the medicine kills me, I wanted you to know. And I'm sorry I got the potion to use on you today. It was wrong."

Potion? He was rambling with fever. "Medicine won't kill you," she told him firmly. "This isn't leeches and bleedings. The doctor will heal you, not hurt you."

She stood. "Now rest. I'm going to get Taylor's keys and bring the car around then I'll come back for you."

Lila and Zach crowded into the cubicle of the time travel machine and stared intently at the monitor.

"There it is!" she crowed. "It worked. Oh my God, it really worked."

"It looks structurally sound, too. It doesn't seem misshapen or warped in any way."

They both stared at the shiny apple from the present lying on top of a bowl of fruit in 1962. The calendar on the wall of a suburban American kitchen verified the year and month—March. Just then a child entered the kitchen door, dropped her school bag on the floor and raced past the table, picking their apple from the bowl as she passed.

"Follow her," Zach said.

Lila fumbled for the controller and tracked the girl from the kitchen into the living room.

The child turned on the TV, changed channels then flopped down on the couch, staring at Little Lulu's antics as she bit into the apple.

"This is unbelievable," Lila murmured, watching the fruit disappear bite by bite into the girl's mouth. "Perfect."

"I'd say a complete success. We transported the apple both where and *when* we wanted it, and the kid's not spitting it out so it must taste okay. I think we can safely send Gareth back to the exact moment from which you took him."

"Well, maybe not exact," she said. "He was in the middle of a battle. I don't want him to get slaughtered because he was distracted."

"First he must be completely well. Imagine if he brought back a flu that wiped out half the world's population."

Lila shuddered. "Don't. It's that kind of idea that's been tying my stomach in knots." She stared at the wholesome picture of a girl watching afternoon cartoons. If she hadn't known it was in another time, it wouldn't have been impressive at all.

Zach's arm brushed Lila's. They were sharing the single seat in the time machine, each with a half-ass hunker that brought their hips and legs in contact. She was aware of the warmth where his thigh pressed against hers.

"Well." He leaned back against his half of the chair. "I hate to bail on you when you're still in the middle of this, but I can't miss another day of work. I have to drive back tonight and teach a class at nine tomorrow morning."

"Oh." Lila was momentarily taken aback. She'd somehow thought he'd be there until Gareth was safely sent home. But Zach had a life of his own, things to do, places to be. She shouldn't have expected he could stay forever. It's just...she was sort of getting used to having him around. "Of course, you should go."

"Here's my cell number." He scribbled it on a piece of paper. "If you need more help or something unexpected comes up, give me a call. Or IM me."

Lila accepted the scrap of paper from Zach. His fingers brushed hers and she remembered what they'd felt like smoothing back her hair, trailing up her spine, delving inside her body. Her stomach tensed as she took the paper. "Thanks. Really, thanks again for everything. I don't know if I could've made it through this without you."

Zach smiled. His pale green eyes shone and his smile was broad and friendly. His cheeks and chin were stubbled from not having shaved in almost two days, but it was a light, blond man's fuzz that actually made him appear younger rather than adding macho. He was simply adorable—not hunky, not alpha male, not commanding, not her type.

Lila inclined toward him, tilting her head and lifting her face. If he wanted to lean down and kiss her, she wouldn't stop him.

But he got up from the chair and moved out of the booth.

Her leg felt cold without his pressed against it. She composed her face into a neutral expression and stood on the other side of the machine. She walked around it and extended her hand to shake his. "Thanks again. I'll keep in touch and tell you what happens."

"Good. Looking forward to it." Zach let go of her hand, went to the door then paused and looked back. "And about the sex, I don't want you to think... I mean, I understand it was just a...one-time thing and I shouldn't have made so much of it. But I wanted to say thanks. It was really nice." He hunched his shoulders a little. "If you ever want to, I don't know, go out again or something, give me a call."

Lila nodded. She didn't know what to say. This was what she'd wanted, right? This was the message she'd given Zach. Friends with occasional benefits.

His tall, gangly frame disappeared through the door.

She opened her mouth to...what? Call after him and ask him to stay? Tell him she didn't mean to be so cold and what they'd done had meant something to her, too? She closed her lips in a tight line. Leaning against the frame of the time machine, she watched little Suzie-whosie get off the couch and wander out of the living room, presumably back to the kitchen for another snack. Lila wondered whose wife, mother, maybe even grandmother the little girl had become. It suddenly made her sad, imagining that girl all grown up with most of her life behind her now.

She flicked off the monitor, wandered over to her work station and sat, elbows on the table, her forehead resting against her palms. The stress and fears of the past two days and her conflicting emotions about Zach were suddenly too much. Her lower lip trembled, her chest rose and fell with suppressed sobs and then two fat teardrops splashed on the tabletop between her elbows. A sad little whimpering sound snuck through her clenched lips. Annoyed at the emotion, Lila wiped furiously at her leaking eyes.

"Hey, chica." Taylor's voice came from the doorway. "I just came up to tell you Chrissy is taking Gareth to the emergency room and... Are you crying?"

"No." Lila blinked the tears away and raised her face to glare at her housemate.

"Huh." Taylor raised a doubtful eyebrow. "Zach just said goodbye and breezed past me. Lover's quarrel?"

"He's not my lover. He's not my anything... Just a friend." Lila turned her attention to straightening her work space. It was a shambles with bits of computer components and papers strewn across it.

"If you say so." She wandered into the room and over to the time machine. "So it's fixed?"

Lila glanced up from her furious straightening. "Yes. And don't touch anything this time."

Taylor held her hands palms up. "Wouldn't dream of it, besides it was Chrissy who screwed up last time, not me. What are you going to do with the machine? I mean, after, and if, you send Gareth home?"

"What do you mean, 'if'?" She set down a stack of papers and faced Taylor.

"I don't think the barbarian is going home. Jeez, why would he want to? Who'd choose freezing winters and

149

outdoor plumbing over climate-controlled weather and hot showers? But most of all there's Chrissy. He's totally in love with her."

Lila had been aware of that on some level, but she'd been so caught up in fixing the machine and in her crush on Zach she hadn't thought about Chrissy and Gareth's escalating relationship. "Well, he can't stay here. He *has* to go back. The repercussions of it... The descendants he won't be there to produce..."

Taylor sat down in the booth and tapped the dark glass on the monitor. "What if Gareth never had any children because he died in that battle we plucked him from? Or what if he stays alone and childless because he never gets over loving Chrissy?"

"But in the original timeline, there wouldn't *be* a Chrissy," Lila protested.

"Maybe this *is* the real timeline. Maybe his story has always gone like this. What's supposed to happen...always happens." She looked at Lila. "And by the way, did you really want Zach to leave without telling him how you feel?"

"What?" Lila frowned. "Where did that come from?"

"Admit it. You like the big puppy-boy. You're hot for him." Taylor lightly fingered the computer keyboard.

"I am not! And stop playing with that."

"Are, too. Was he that good in bed?" Taylor's eyes glinted mischievously.

Lila paused too long.

Taylor jumped on the telling silence and began teasing unmercifully. "He was! He was an amazing lovah, and now you can't stand to let him go."

"Shut up. Don't be an ass."

Taylor's grin gentled to a smile. "Go after him, Lila. If you really like the guy, what are you waiting for? I've realized lately messing around with a lot of men is fun and all, but it gets old. Actually connecting with someone on a deep, emotional level is...really rare."

Lila stared. She'd never heard Taylor sound so sincere. Usually the girl played her self-created role of bubble-headed blonde to the max. "I..."

"You what? You *don't* like him? You don't want him? The pair of you aren't one hundred percent compatible with your ginormous brains? What are you afraid of, Lila-belle?"

"I don't know," Lila whispered. "I'm... Do you think he's gone yet? I mean driven away?"

"Find out. Call him and tell him to wait."

Lila flew down the stairs and through the front hall, snatching up her cell phone and dialing as she ran out the front door and down the sidewalk.

Zach had been forced to park almost a block away from their house and she searched the darkness for the white shape of his Saturn. She was just in time to see red taillights as the little car pulled out onto the street.

She darted after it like a commuter chasing a bus, then slowed to a walk after a few yards as it turned the corner. His phone stopped ringing and his voice came on. "Hi. It's Zach. Please leave a message."

There was a pause then a beep. Lila sucked in a breath. "It's me. I..." She grasped for the right words. "I'm sorry I was such a bitch to you after we... I really like you and I do want to get together and... Call me." She stabbed the End button before she could fumble it any worse. "Damn."

After standing on the sidewalk a moment, staring down the street, she turned to walk back to the house. She hadn't gone more than a yard before her phone rang. She almost dropped it in her haste to answer. "Hello?"

"Lila?" Zach's voice was warm as sunshine. "I saw you called."

"Where are you?"

"A few streets away from your house. What's up? Another emergency?"

"No. I mean, yes. Kinda. I just... I didn't want you to leave before I told you... God, this is hard." She exhaled and started again. "I know I was an ass after we had sex, acting like it didn't mean anything to me. But it did. I've never been so... It was more than just sex. It was making love and it...it meant something. I guess that scared me. I'm not used to feeling so deeply, you know? I'm always thinking about how things work and why and applying logic to every situation. For me to feel something so strong and sudden and inexplicable and not be able to control what I'm feeling is frighten... Oh!" Lila stopped short.

Zach had gone around the block. His car pulled up to the curb a few yards in front of her. He got out, holding his phone to his ear. "I'm listening," he said as he stepped up on the sidewalk. Then he turned off the phone and approached her.

Lila hesitated. It was easier to talk into the phone than face Zach's searching eyes and say what she wanted to say. She tilted her head to look up at him.

The streetlights glinted off his eyes and cast his face in sharp relief. In the harsh light with a serious expression on his face, he looked much less boyish. He was all man.

Her stomach clenched and her pulse rabbited. "I guess I already said everything. I like you as a friend, yes, but more than that, I lo..." She choked on the word, not ready to admit it. "I really *like* you like you, in a boyfriend kind of way."

A smile spread over his face. His teeth gleamed in the glow from the streetlight. "I like you like you, too, Lila." He drew her into his arms and brought his face close to hers, but didn't kiss her. "I liked you when we were just internet pals, but after I saw you—whew, there was no doubt."

"God, it seems so illogical. Me and you being so different. And the long distance thing—"

"Shhh." He covered her mouth with his to stop her words. When he pulled his soft lips away again, Lila had forgotten why she was protesting.

"We're not so different," Zach said. "And we'll work out the long distance issues. An hour and a half isn't that far. Besides, I'll be finished with my dissertation soon and after I graduate I can move closer if we're still... If things progress."

Progress, Lila thought. *Into what? Marriage?* She felt herself starting to fret again. To stop her brain from thinking too hard, she rose up on her toes and kissed him again. This time they clung together for long moments, their mouths fusing hungrily.

Zach's hot, wet tongue plumbed the depths of her mouth, exploring the ridges of her palate and coiling around her tongue. She did the same, her tongue performing acrobatics as it twisted with his. Her hands slid up his chest and clutched his shoulders. Her fingers stole around the back of his neck and fondled the ends of his silky hair. His neck was warm and solid and his hair so very soft it made her sigh into his mouth.

She moved sinuously against Zach's long, tall body, eager to feel every inch of him touching her. Her crotch slid against his groin and he thrust toward her, clutching her ass and pulling her tight against him. The street was dark except for the streetlights and the yellow squares of windows in the row of houses. There was no one to see them dry-humping right there on the sidewalk.

"Holy shit," he panted when they finally pulled apart.

She, too, was breathless. "Do you have to leave right now? Maybe we could take a few minutes and..."

He nodded. "Yeah. Definitely have time," he said hoarsely.

Lila's pussy ached and clenched at the raw desire in his voice. She rubbed her crotch against him again and moaned softly. "Mmm. My room or your car?"

"Car's closer," he mumbled against her neck. His lips nuzzled from her jaw down to her collarbone. His hand slid up to her breast and squeezed lightly through her shirt.

"Car it is," she agreed, offering her throat like a woman hoping for a vampire's bite. His mouth settled in the hollow of her throat and she wondered if he could feel her pulse pounding against his tongue.

"Come on." Zach's voice was so deep and rasping it barely sounded like him. He grabbed her hand and pulled her toward where his car was parked.

Grasping his big, warm hand tightly, she looked up at the tall, shaggy-haired, white boy beside her. It was funny how quickly your ideal man could change.

Chapter Nine

Taylor stared at the screen. There he was—the man of her dreams. Holy shit, he was hot!

He was walking along the sidewalk through a crowd of people, briefcase in hand, headed to work or home from work or maybe to a business meeting. It was like the man had a halo around him. He shone. He stood out from the crowd. The sun made his pale blond hair glow. He turned his head to look at something in a shop window and his profile was strong and masculine contrasting with full, almost feminine, bite-able lips.

"I could suck that bottom lip like a pacifier." Taylor maneuvered the control to keep up with her chosen target. When a passing couple temporarily blocked her view of the man, she swore, and when he reappeared in all his glorious maleness, she froze the image. "There! Gotcha, hottie!"

She examined him at her leisure. He filled the shoulders of his jacket like a store mannequin. His suit was well-tailored and fit his trim body perfectly. He could have been strolling the catwalk, he carried himself with such elegant grace.

Taylor zoomed in on his face. Hottie McHott had clear blue eyes with long dark eyelashes, arched eyebrows drawn into a slight frown, a strong jaw, straight nose and, oh by the way, fucking *bite-able*, full, pouting lips. And, of course, the early-Brad Pitt blond hair that flopped across his forehead and straggled a little over his crisp, white shirt collar.

She reminded herself the point in picking a guy from the future was not for his hotness, but because he'd be more sensitive and evolved then the current flavor of jerks she'd been dating. "I'm gonna love you for your big brain and enlightened attitudes, honey, but that bottom lip sure doesn't hurt."

Her hand hesitated over the button. She thought about how Lila was going to kill her and how she might fuck up time or something, although she hadn't noticed any changes in the world since they'd brought Gareth forward. How could taking a guy from the future possibly hurt anything? She pressed the button. "Come to Mama, sweetheart."

There was a high-pitched whining sound and static electricity swept through the small booth. It stood her hair on end, prickling her scalp and lifting the tiny hairs on her arms. At the same time it was like a vacuum had sucked all the air out of the room.

The blond Adonis appeared in the booth right next to her. He was still in motion, as though walking down the city street. His briefcase banged into Taylor's shoulder, knocking her sideways in the chair.

"Ouch, fuck!" She grabbed her arm and stood, scooting out of his way.

Hottie bumped into the monitor then froze, registering his change in location. "What...?" His mouth stayed open. He blinked, then his eyes opened so wide the whites showed all around the sapphire irises. His gaze darted from the booth to the room to her and he cried out, stumbling a step backward and dropping the briefcase.

"It's okay." She raised her hands, palms open. "You're all right."

"What happened? Where am I?"

"Hi, my name is Taylor. This is a time machine. You're in the past," Taylor gave her pre-rehearsed speech. "2007, to be exact. This is a scientific experiment. Think of it as a chance for you to see living history. Although I have to say there are probably more interesting time periods you could visit than this one."

Golden Boy took another step backward, staring at Taylor, taking her in from head to toe.

"The fashion's probably a little dated, huh?" She suddenly felt self-conscious. "That's why I chose you from only sixty years in the future. I didn't want society to have changed too much. From what I've seen, the styles don't look all that different." She stepped back in the booth and gestured at the monitor.

The handsome man moved in close and peered over her shoulder at the frozen picture on the screen. It was the same city street from which he'd been removed. Taylor pressed a button and the pedestrians resumed walking.

"What have you done to me?" he whispered, reaching out a hand but pausing just short of touching the monitor.

"What's your name?" She tried to calm him down with her best patient-soothing voice.

He didn't answer, continuing to stare at the monitor then looking around the room again liked a trapped animal.

Taylor rested a hand on his arm. "It's all right. We can send you back after a while. Think of this as the biggest adventure you'll ever have."

He looked down into her eyes, frowning. "Who are you? Why would you do this? Is it some kind of government experiment?" He pulled his arm away from her hand.

"My name is Taylor," she repeated, "and yours is...?"

He hesitated then finally said, "John. John Wilkins."

"Seriously? John? I thought sixty years from now people would have more exotic names. You know, like romance novel names."

He stared at her as if she was insane.

"Anyway I'm not government. My friend, Lila, is an inventor. She came up with this." Taylor gestured at the booth. "A couple of days ago we accidentally brought a guy forward from ancient times. He's still here, as a matter of fact. I don't think he'll be going home 'cause he fell in love with my friend, Chrissy. I thought it would be interesting to talk to someone from the future before Lila destroys the time machine for the good of mankind, so I brought you here."

"Are you crazy? You can't play with people's lives like this!"

"It'll be okay. I'll put you right back when I got you from." Taylor glanced down at the moving image on the monitor and it suddenly occurred to her that she should have left it frozen. "Or close to it." She quickly clicked the button and stopped the image again.

John's bewilderment gave way to anger. "I had a very important client to meet this afternoon. This is...impossible, irresponsible! Where is the woman who invented this thing?"

"Um, Lila's running after her boyfriend to tell him how she feels. She should be back soon." Taylor squinted. "Are you a lawyer?" A starched-shirt, uptight, workaholic attorney wasn't what she'd had in mind. She could find plenty of those today.

He frowned. "No. Why would you assume that?"

"You said you were meeting a client so I thought—"

"I'm a systems analyst for Globalcon Internacionale."

"Oh my God, a corporate drone! It's worse than I thought. How many hours a week do you work?"

"Why are you asking me these things?" John whirled away from her and strode across the room toward Lila's work station, where he examined the schematic still pinned to the corkboard above it. "If your friend really invented this machine, if I really am in the past, why don't we have this technology in my time?"

"I told you. She's going to destroy it." Taylor followed him across the room. "You know, you're not going to miss any work, so you can quit worrying about it. Think of this as a vacation."

"I don't take vacations." He straightened and looked down at her with cool blue eyes.

"A day off, then."

"I don't take those either."

"Never?" She moved in close to him, determined to catch his attention. She cocked her head, eyes wide and lips slightly pouted. Taylor had been winning boys' hearts like trophies since she was twelve years old. She knew how to attract a man, but he seemed immune to her flirtation.

"No. I'm on the Dorancian Program." He stared at her without any of the telltale signs of arousal—the dilation of the pupils, the quickened breath, the flushed face.

"You're on the what, now?" Taylor swayed back and forth a little with her chest thrust forward. Nothing.

"I take Dorancian. I don't do vacations and days off." His tone was arrogant.

"Um, please explain this to an ignorant historical figure."

"Dr. Arthur Dorancian invented the drug in 2033. It enhances work performance by suppressing the libido or desire for extra-curricular activities. It ensures single-mindedness concentration on work. Executives who're serious about their career are on the Program—at least until they're successful and ready to take the time to procreate."

"You're shittin' me. Reverse Viagra? That's unbelievable. All for a career?"

"Dorancian has reduced overpopulation worldwide. It's one of the most important inventions of the last century." John stopped speaking and shook his head. "Why are we even talking about this? I demand you send me back where I came from right now."

"Wait. I have to hear more about this." *Besides, I don't know how to work the machine in reverse.* Taylor rested a hand on his arm again.

He stared at it with hard eyes until she removed it.

"So, tell me, when you decide you're ready...to procreate, how long does it take for the drug to get out of your system and your, uh, desires to return?"

"If you miss a dose two days in a row, the effects are obvious and by the end of five days the drug is totally cleared from your system."

"Does lust come flooding in all at once, or bit by bit?"

John reddened and turned away. "I don't have time to discuss this. I need to get back."

"Honey, you've got all the time in the world." She trailed after him across the room to the window overlooking several city blocks. "Besides, I, uh, don't know how it works. We have to wait for Lila to return. Meanwhile, why don't you come downstairs? I'll show you around the house and we could get to know each other."

"I..." John hesitated, fingering the curtain at the window and gazing at the nighttime view of the city. "It would be interesting to see the antiques."

"Antiques, right." Taylor took his hand and pulled him toward the door. "Come on. I'll make you some old-fashioned food in the kitchen." As she led him downstairs, Taylor thought her plan might work after all. For once she'd spend time getting to know a guy, a man with no sexual desire for her, someone she could talk to without him having the ulterior motive of getting in her pants.

And then, in a couple of days, after she'd proven to herself she could have a simple friendship with a man, he'd be ready to rut like an elk. Taylor shivered at the thought of golden John without his tailored suit on.

All she needed was an excuse to keep him around for a few days.

John had never met anyone like Taylor. She was so...light. One might say shallow, the way she chattered incessantly about unimportant things. She had no more thought for consequences than a child. That's what she reminded him of, a child, except for her soft, curvy, very mature body.

He frowned and turned his attention away from her form. He hadn't taken his Dorancian yet today. He'd missed his morning dose, planning to refill the prescription in the afternoon. Already he could feel the faint stirrings of sensations he'd laid to rest several years ago when he went on the Program. He was experiencing not only the prickle of interest in the pretty woman, but a surge of hunger for the fragrant dish she'd placed in front of him. Ravenously, he dug into the plate of meatless lasagna.

"See. I told you you'd be hungry once you started eating. I figure if air travel takes it out of you, time travel must do the same."

There it was again, her skewed logic. She looked at things with a sort of naiveté that made sense in its own way. "Thank you. It's very good." John's gaze slid from the plate in front of him to Taylor bustling around the kitchen, straightening and cleaning.

"I never know who's going to eat at home, so when it's my turn to cook, I try to make things that taste just as good re-heated." She laughed and the sound was as light and tinkling as the upper range of a piano. "Who am I kidding? It's *always* my turn to cook. Lila and Chrissy would order takeout every day if it weren't for me."

"Can you tell me about the year we're in? Refresh me on my history."

Taylor sat across the table from him. "Oh my God, this is history to you! I mean, I knew it was, but it's so weird. You're really taking this very well."

John forked the last bite of pasta from his plate. "In my time, they're on the verge of perfecting teleporters for transportation. It seems to me there's little difference in traveling through space or time."

"Wow! What else do you have in the future? I didn't see any flying cars, although I suppose you wouldn't need them if you're going to have teleporters. Do you still have movies? How about dance clubs? I love dancing. And concerts. What kind of music do you listen to?"

John's head spun from Taylor's abrupt conversational twists. "Classical."

"Really? I like songs with words. I like to sing along." She leaned forward on her elbows, regarding him. "Do you sing or play any instruments?"

John thought about the glossy black Steinway at his grandmother's house, the hours of solitary practice in the afternoons. "I used to play piano." He hadn't thought about it for years.

"Used to? Why did you stop?"

"I wasn't good enough," he admitted.

Taylor frowned, her pale eyebrows drawing together over bright blue eyes. "Why would that stop you from playing?"

"There was no point to it. When the teacher told her I would never be concert hall material, my mother cancelled the lessons."

"That's terrible! Music is supposed to be fun. You could have played for your own enjoyment. I was never good in my tap classes either, but it hasn't stopped me from dancing." Taylor was obviously prepared to say more, but the phone rang. "Just a sec." She jumped up and left the kitchen.

John gazed around the room at the antique appliances with their clunky, boxy shapes. He rose and took his bowl to the sink. "Water on," he said, but nothing

Bonnie Dee

happened. He had to manually turn on the tap to rinse the bowl. "Lights off." He tested the lights and they didn't respond either. "Amazing." He walked over to the switch on the wall and turned it off and on a couple of times.

Taylor re-appeared in the doorway. "Well, that was Lila, the one who invented the time machine. She's not going to be back until late tomorrow afternoon."

"What?" Real fear lanced through John as he realized he was actually trapped here, that this was really happening and wouldn't be over soon.

"Yeah. She's going to her boyfriend's house tonight. They just got together and she wants to check out where he lives. He'll bring her back tomorrow evening. This is very impulsive for Lila. She said she needed a break after everything that's happened over the past two days."

"What?" He repeated. "Did you tell her about me?"

Taylor's gaze shifted away. "Lila was so happy and I figured another day wouldn't make that much difference. Aren't you interested in seeing old-fashioned Chicago by daylight? I have a shift, but I can call in sick and take you around sight-seeing all day tomorrow."

"You're crazy. Absolutely insane. Call your friend back and tell her I need to get home. I have a life and responsibilities and..." John sputtered to an end. It was pointless to rail at her. Taylor continued to gaze at him with those guileless, what'd-I-do, blue eyes.

"Calm down." She approached him and laid her hand on his arm again. "Take it easy and try to enjoy your visit."

Her hand was warm. John had removed his jacket and could feel the warmth through the thin cotton of his shirt. He inhaled her sweet, floral perfume and felt a twitching sensation in his groin. Even after she removed her hand, there was a tingling on his arm where she'd touched him. He forgot everything he'd intended to say.

"Let me get you a drink. You need to unwind after all you've been through." Taylor went to one of the kitchen cupboards and stood on her tiptoes to get a bottle from the top shelf.

John eyed her bottom, stretching and wiggling, and felt the twitchy stirring inside him once more. The effects of the Dorancian were wearing off sooner than he would have expected. He really needed to get home and take a pill. His head jerked up at the sound of the front door opening and a voice calling, "Hello. We're back."

"In the kitchen," Taylor answered. She turned to John, a bottle dangling from her hand. "I don't suppose you could pretend to be one of my co-workers who dropped by for a drink." She sighed. "Ah, what the hell. Chrissy's going to find out sooner or later, I might as well get the bitching over with."

A moment later, a redhead and a large, bearded, black-haired man appeared in the doorway. The woman's arm was around the man, whose breathing was labored. He leaned into her, appearing groggy.

John stared in amazement at the living, breathing antiquity Taylor had told him about. Gareth didn't look like a medieval barbarian. He looked like a regular guy.

Chrissy stared back at John. "Who's your friend, Taylor?" she asked in a "What are you thinking of inviting strangers over to the house?" kind of way.

"Oh, don't worry about John," Taylor said breezily. "He knows everything."

"What?"

"He knows about Gareth. How is the big lug, by the way? He looks worse than ever."

"The doctor said it's a flu and there's nothing to do but wait it out. He prescribed an antibiotic to get rid of any secondary infection." Chrissy shifted under the heavy arm the big man had slung over her shoulders. "Taylor, who is this and why did you tell him about—"

"Promise not to yell," Taylor interrupted. "His name is John Wilkins. He's from the year 2067, here for a visit. Surprise!"

"What have you done?" Chrissy's eyes opened wide.

John was glad to hear someone respond in an appropriate manner to Taylor's carelessness. The woman had almost convinced him he was being uptight about the whole thing.

"Your friend, Taylor, is crazy," Gareth said to Chrissy while observing John curiously.

"Thank you. Exactly what I thought," John said.

"You understood him?" Taylor turned to John. "What did he say?"

"Of course, I understood him. A translator's essential for global business."

"Translator," Chrissy repeated. "You're wearing one now. Does it look anything like this?" She removed a small device from her ear and showed it to John.

He walked over and looked at it. "No. I have a Janzen cochlear implant. It translates thought patterns, not languages."

"That's Lila's last name!" Taylor exclaimed. "Her invention—it's there, in the future. She'll be so excited."

"Janzen—*that's* your friend Lila?" John looked more closely at the translator. "And this is a prototype. Unbelievable! This is one of the most important inventions in the history of the world. It's been the key to achieving stability between nations."

"Wow." Taylor blew out a breath. "We're living with friggin' Einstein."

John handed the device back to Chrissy. "Janzen just..." He bit back the words that almost came from his mouth. "She's a genius. I can't wait to actually meet her." He looked at the famous inventor's two roommates. There was no reason to tell the women that their friend, Lila Janzen-Meyer, died November 5, 2065 at age eighty-four.

"Where *is* Lila?" Chrissy asked.

"With Zach in Wellington. She'll be back later," Taylor said.

Gareth coughed, his breath rattling in his chest.

Chrissy glanced at him. "All right, Taylor. You sort out your own mess and deal with the wrath of Lila. I've got to get this guy to bed." She nodded at John. "Nice meeting you and I'm so sorry about Taylor. She's more than a little impulsive." She wrapped an arm around Gareth's back and the couple left the room.

"Well..." Taylor turned to John and held up the bottle of whiskey. "How 'bout that drink now?"

John rarely drank. He wasn't used to it and didn't know why he accepted the glass of whiskey from Taylor. As the amber liquid burned down his throat to settle warmly in his stomach, he found himself saying things to her he hadn't admitted to anyone, least of all himself. Maybe it was something about being in a place where no one knew him or had expectations of him, but as the minutes ticked by and his head began to buzz from the alcohol, John talked.

"It wasn't my life's ambition to work for Globalcon, stuck behind a desk all day except when I'm dealing with clients. It just happened." He swirled the whiskey around in his glass, enjoying the undulations of color in the liquid. He tried to blink the fog from his brain. "I needed... Actually, my mother needed the security Globalcon provides. I didn't have anything better in mind, so I took the job she suggested. I'm making an insane amount of money and I'm on the fast track to partnership." He took a sip of the whiskey and laughed sharply. "It was just a job. Now it's my life."

"That's dumb." Taylor tapped the side of her glass with her pink-painted nails. "No one should have a job that doesn't make them happy." She pointed at him. "*You* need to think about what you really want to do with your life, and then...do it."

"Easy to say." He downed the rest of the whiskey in a gulp.

"Easy to do, too. You're not married, right? No dependents, no one except your mom counting on you financially. Now's the time in your life to make a change. Find out who you want to be." Taylor smiled and her eyes sparkled, mesmerizing him. "Play the piano again."

He didn't answer. She made it sound easy, but he'd been following other people's plans for his life for so long, he thought maybe he'd forgotten how to choose for himself.

She stood and took the empty glass from his hand. "Think about it, but, meanwhile, come with me."

John looked at her with raised eyebrows, but she didn't offer an explanation. She put the glasses in the sink and led him from the room.

"I told you I'm a physical therapist. I'm also a trained massage therapist." Taylor cast a glance over her shoulder as they walked toward the stairs. "And, honey, I've never met anyone more in need of a relaxing massage than you."

John swallowed hard, imagining her hands sliding over his skin and pressing into his muscles. A massage sounded good—better than good. His body ached for her to touch it. As he ascended the stairs, his head felt fuzzy, his tongue thick, and he realized for the first time in years he was well on his way to drunk. He clutched the banister to keep his balance and followed Taylor the rest of the way upstairs.

Her bedroom was just like the woman, soft, feminine and floral-scented. There were discarded clothes, high-heeled shoes, bits of lacy underwear and filmy bras scattered across the floor. A pink lava lamp glowed in the corner as a nightlight. The flowery bedcovers were rumpled. Ivory satin sheets straggled halfway onto the floor.

Taylor crossed the room, quickly pulled the covers straight and plumped the pillows. Then she looked over at John and patted the bed. "Sit down."

He licked his numb lips and obeyed, sitting stiffly on the edge of the bed.

Taylor dropped to her knees and removed his socks and shoes. "Let your feet breathe." She grinned up at him.

The sight of her kneeling at his feet made his stomach flip in a pleasant way and his cock twitch and stir again.

Taylor stood and climbed onto the bed to kneel behind him.

John sat still, barely breathing, as she rested her hands on his shoulders.

"Just let yourself relax for once." Her warm breath tickled his ear. Her hands dug into his shoulder muscles, kneading and pulling the tension out of them with long, hard strokes.

His eyes drifted closed and he suppressed a groan of pleasure. The alcohol heated his stomach, suffusing him with a peaceful euphoria.

Taylor's hands moved around to his chest and began unbuttoning his shirt.

John's eyes flew open. "What are you...?"

"A massage works better if you're shirtless. Trust me," she said. "I'm a physical therapist. I work with people's bodies all the time."

Before John could protest, Taylor had stripped off his shirt.

He didn't try to stop her. He sat there half-naked, his nipples pebbling in the cool air of her bedroom, as her hands roamed over his body.

"Lie on your stomach now," she commanded in a throaty murmur that sent a shiver through him. "I'll get my massage oil."

John felt pliant as a child as he obediently stretched out face down on the soft bed. There were rustling sounds behind him then Taylor was back, straddling his hips and perching on his ass. The weight and warmth of her buttocks and thighs wrapped around him. A second later her hands, slick with oil, rubbed his shoulders again. The scent of lavender rose to his nose.

"Lavender's a healing plant, good for calming the nervous system," Taylor explained as she stroked and kneaded his shoulders. Her hands were strong and her touch firm, as she worked her way down his back.

John hadn't realized his muscles stored so much tension until Taylor released it. She found tender spots that made him groan and flinch as she rubbed briskly.

"Don't be such a baby." She pressed deeply right between his shoulderblades. "You have to release your stress. Let it go and the pain will go with it." Sure enough, as Taylor continued to knead the sore muscles, the tightness released and the pain diminished. Her hands were like magic.

His eyes closed again as he rode the waves of sensations her touch brought. The massage was more than physically therapeutic. No one had touched John in a long time. His life revolved around work almost eighteen hours a day. He hadn't realized he missed human contact until he felt this woman's hands moving over his flesh, freeing tension and long-buried emotions. Despite the suppressing effect of the Dorancian, there was a carnal element to the feelings flooding John's system. He was aroused and his cock stirred in a way it hadn't for almost five years. He shifted as his erection grew, pressing into the mattress beneath him.

"You're obviously spending way too much time at a computer keyboard. I've never felt muscles so stiff."

He smiled into the pillow. "Keyboards were phased out over a decade ago. Computers are all vocal now. As a matter of fact, most things run on voice commands."

"Really? Just like in sci-fi movies. Cool." Taylor's hands reached John's lower back. He was very aware of their proximity to his ass as she vigorously kneaded just above his buttocks then slipped lower, under the waistband of his pants. His groin glowed warmly—probably from the alcohol, he decided. "You know, if you like I can keep going. Give you a full body massage. I'm sure there's a lot of tension in your legs as well."

"No, thank you. That's all right." He was determined to keep his pants on.

"Well, all right. But I'm telling you, I can help." She smoothed her hands up his back all the way to his shoulders again then began working on his arms.

John gasped as she dug into his biceps with determination.

"Uh-huh." She grunted, pressing hard. "You may not spend time hunched over a keyboard, but your arms and shoulders are still way tight."

He winced but went with the pain, riding it until it turned into pleasure. The tension released and his arms felt loose and light. He sighed.

Taylor worked her hands busily up and down his right arm, then his left, squeezing his biceps and forearms and rotating each shoulder in its socket. "Roll over," she commanded when she was finished. He felt her weight lift from his ass.

Compliantly, he obeyed, lying on his back looking up at her.

She sat on the bed beside him, legs curled beneath her, and reached for his hand. Taking it between her soft palms, she massaged each of his fingers. When she had manipulated all ten digits, she pressed her fingertips into his palms, locating pressure points and working them. Her head was bent to her task and he could examine her freely without fear of being caught staring.

Taylor had beautiful eyelashes. Long and lush, they brushed against her cheekbones as she looked down. John watched them flutter when she blinked. Hazily, he wanted to touch them with his finger to see if they were soft, wanted to feel them brush his skin with butterfly kisses on his chest, his stomach, his thighs. Once more his cock stirred with life at the image of her batting her eyelashes against his skin and pressing kisses on his flesh.

Taylor's hair was curly, shiny and golden, a shade darker than his own. A lock of her hair had fallen over her eyes and John clenched his fingers to keep from reaching out to tuck it behind her ear.

Her lips were a luscious shade of pink; the lower was full and there was a deep bow in the upper one. They pursed slightly as she massaged the back of his right hand then trailed her fingers lightly up and down it.

John shivered at the erotic touch of her fingernails scratching his skin.

She looked at him and her eyes were almost a neon shade of blue. "Cold?"

"N-no." His teeth were almost chattering. The shivers on his spine were growing unbearable and his cock... How could it be so hard? He'd only missed one pill.

Taylor continued to gaze deep into his eyes as she massaged his other hand.

He couldn't look away and felt like a fly trapped by a spider. Except he didn't struggle in her web and he wanted to be eaten. He imagined his cock being engulfed in that pretty pink mouth, and swallowed with an audible click of his throat.

Placing his hand gently by his side and never breaking eye contact, she braced a hand on either side of his shoulders and leaned down toward him.

He held his breath as her face drew close, filling his vision. Her soft lips touched his, pressing lightly against them. His eyes closed as his mouth parted in response to their warm wetness. Taylor's lips pressed more firmly against his and her tongue delicately probed his mouth.

Pulse racing, he kissed her back. He should have felt no stirring of desire, but his body was clearly drug-free enough to respond to her kisses. He wrapped his arms around her and held her soft, curvaceous body, running his hands up and down her back and feeling the texture of her fuzzy sweater that tickled his naked chest.

Taylor leaned into him harder, her body pinning him to the bed. She moved her leg over his hips and straddled him, her crotch gently rubbing against the growing bulge in the front of his pants.

John felt like he was floating underwater. His head swam and her movements on top of him were languorous and easy. He threaded his fingers through her silky blonde curls and cradled her delicate skull. His tongue swirled inside her mouth, slipping over hers. His body responded as a man's body should to a beautiful woman writhing on top of him, heart rate up and erection steadily rising. He was glad because it would be embarrassing if...

Suddenly things came to a grinding halt. The time-released Dorancian must have kicked in because John's surging manhood flagged and faded. The emotions that had been churning through his system sputtered and died, replaced by an all too familiar coolness and detachment.

Taylor pulled her mouth from his. "What's wrong?"

"Nothing. I just...I'm not interested."

"Oh." Her bottom lip thrust out a little in an annoyed pout. "Is it that drug or me?"

"The drug, definitely," John assured her. "You're fine." He rubbed her back so she wouldn't feel bad. "And I'm a little overwhelmed by being pulled through time and by the whiskey. I told you I don't drink."

"So you want to sleep now?"

"I am kind of tired."

She rolled off of him and flopped on her back with a little sigh. "You're right. You should rest."

"Thanks for the massage," John offered as an apology for his non-performance.

"No problem. Glad to help. Maybe by tomorrow you'll be up for...some sightseeing in the city."

"Yes. I'd enjoy that." He yawned, feeling dozy from the alcohol and the deep body massage. "I can sleep on your couch."

"No. Here is fine. I promise not to molest you."

John thought he heard her whisper, "Much," before he drifted off to sleep.

Chrissy lay beside Gareth, watching him sleep.

Spikes of hair clung damply to his forehead. Behind his eyelids, his eyes moved rapidly back and forth, scanning unknown images.

She stroked the hair away from his forehead, noting that his fever had broken.

Shifting beneath her touch, he mumbled something and batted her hand away from his face.

She smiled and laid her hand back on the bed. Her eyes prickled with unshed tears and her stomach ached as she realized she was going to have to let him go. As soon as he was well enough, he must be returned to his own time, not for the sake of the continuity of history, but for his own good.

His body wasn't equipped to deal with the germs and diseases of the twenty-first century. This time he'd only had a minor flu, but next time he might catch diphtheria or mumps or some other long-extinct disease which could kill him. Gareth had to go back where he belonged.

But the only way he would leave her now was if she convinced him she didn't care. She would work on that...starting tomorrow.

Taylor watched John sleep. She hoped he didn't have a hangover tomorrow, but at least between the alcohol and the massage he was finally relaxed.

She'd enjoyed talking with him and really enjoyed kissing him. And strangely enough, considering she'd only known him a few hours, she finally felt that elusive connection she'd been searching for. Beneath his handsome exterior was a sad and vulnerable person she wanted to get to know better, but she needed more time.

Tomorrow, when he was sober, he'd be fretting to be returned home again. She only had one short day to win him over and convince him to stay for a while, and to convince Lila. Unless...

Taylor imagined smashing the time machine, effectively trapping both John and Gareth until Lila fixed the damn thing again. She mentally shook her head. No, even she wasn't that selfish.

Stretching out on her side beside John, she tucked an arm under her head and watched the beautiful man sleep—and listened to him snore. Various scenarios in which she convinced him to stay played out in her head. She just needed a little more time with him.

All she needed was a couple more days.

Lila came back from the bathroom and stood beside the bed a moment watching Zach sleep. His chest rose and fell with deep, steady breaths.

She'd never done anything in her life as impulsive as going away with Zach for the night. It was so irresponsible of her, especially leaving Chrissy to deal with Gareth's illness. She didn't even want to think about her job, which she might not have anymore. She'd called in sick every day this week. Sitting on the edge of the bed, she smoothed her hand over Zach's naked chest, feeling his heartbeat thumping under her palm. Not having a job might not be so bad. If she wanted to, she could relocate here, live closer to Zach—maybe even live *with* Zach eventually. She could work on her projects anywhere. Maybe she could even get a grant from the university and have her work completely funded.

Lying down beside him, she curled close to his side, breathing in the scent of his skin. For a few moments she spun the pleasant daydream of their future together, then her mind abruptly bumped to earth as she remembered the matter of her invention was still unresolved.

Before planning anything for her own future, she must return Gareth home, dismantle the machine and store the blueprints and data in a safe deposit box somewhere. Lila sighed as she realized she was planning to scrap years' worth of hard work. It wasn't going to be easy to give up her dream, but for the safety of the world she must abandon her project.

Tomorrow, when she got home, if Gareth's health was better she'd send him home and destroy her masterpiece.

Up in Lila's workroom, the time machine's monitor still glowed, frozen on the city scene where Taylor had left it. But the picture had changed.

The street was bleak and half empty, the buildings dirty and smoke-stained. Some were spray-painted with graffiti: "Resist! Never surrender!" Other buildings were mere piles of rubble—brick and mortar and jutting iron beams making surrealistic sculptures. Smoke floated over the scene, shrouding it in hazy gray.

The few people in the scene were frozen in the act of darting from the safety of one building to another. Their clothes were worn and their faces pinched with fear and strain. They were the faces of war.

As the hours before dawn slipped away, three pairs of lovers slept peacefully and the fate of the world's future hung poised in doubt.

Chapter Ten

Taylor woke spooned against the warm body of a man. She shifted and snuggled contentedly beneath John's sleep-heavy arm and listened to his deep, steady breathing. She could get used to this.

But a moment later he woke with a start, lifting his arm from her and shifting away. "Sorry. I didn't mean to..."

What an ignorant ass! Couldn't he tell she *wanted* to be cuddled next to him? "It's all right." Taylor rolled onto her back to face him. "Slept pretty good, huh?"

"Yes." A flush crept from his neck and his eyes wouldn't meet hers. He sat, pushing the covers off and looked around the room.

"Your shirt's on the floor." Taylor watched his back muscles ripple as he rose from the bed. Remembering how smooth and hot his skin felt beneath her hands last night, her pussy clenched with desire. She wanted more of him and was determined that before the day was over, she'd have it.

When John extended his arms over his head to slip on his white T-shirt, his taut stomach stretched and his hard little nipples rose high.

Ooh, she wanted to lick and bite those nipples.

He glanced at her and Taylor glanced away from his body, flustered to be caught gawking. "Hmm? What did you say?"

"I didn't say anything." He frowned and picked up his dress shirt. "But I was thinking we should call Lila Janzen and ask her to come back as soon as possible, so I can get home."

A loud knock on the door made them both jump.

"Taylor!" Chrissy threw the door open without waiting for an answer and stalked into the room. "You never *told* Lila about John? She just called to see how Gareth is doing and now she wants to talk to you." Chrissy held the cell phone out.

Taylor took it and held it gingerly to her ear. "Hello?"

Lila started right in. "Taylor, I can't believe this! That machine is not a catalog for you to choose men from. It's not a toy box where you can pick your own personal Ken doll! What the hell were you thinking?"

"No harm done. You and Zach tested the machine. You can send both John and Gareth back whenever, right?"

"I hope so, but... Oh, never mind. It's hopeless talking to you. Just sit tight and don't touch any more buttons. I'm borrowing Zach's car, dropping him on campus, then I'll be on my way home." The line went dead.

Taylor handed Chrissy's phone back to her. "Lila's coming."

"Good," John and Chrissy said in unison.

Taylor sighed. There went her hopes of a long, leisurely day with John.

When Chrissy returned to her room, Gareth was awake and sitting up in bed, his black hair a tangled mess and his torso arousingly naked. "Gud morrrnink, Chrissy," he said in English. He smiled, pleased at his pronunciation.

Her heart clenched in her chest like a big knobby fist. "Morning," she responded briefly without a smile. "You're feeling better?"

"Yesss," he replied, continuing to use the English she'd taught him.

"That's good. I'll get you another pill in a minute. You have to take all of the antibiotics." She crossed the room to her dresser and grabbed clothes from the drawer.

"What is the matter?" Gareth asked in his own tongue.

There was a creak behind her as he rose from the bed. She had to get out of the room fast before he touched her and her resolve crumbled. "Nothing." She turned to go to the bathroom to dress, but a mountain of man-flesh stood in her way.

He cupped her chin in his hand and tilted her face. "What's wrong?"

She forced herself to meet his gaze. "Lila's on her way back. When she gets here she'll send you back so you should probably wear your own clothes today."

"I don't wish to go." He stared down at her gravely.

"I want you to." Chrissy gazed unblinking into his dark eyes. "You don't belong here. I have a life and you're not part of it. I want you to go home." The pain in her heart made the words come out as harsh as they must be to convince Gareth.

He caressed her jaw with his fingers and searched her eyes for the truth. "Chrissy?"

She kept her expression neutral as she spoke past the lump in her throat. "I had a good time with you. The sex was wonderful. But it's time for you to go back where you belong." He stared into her eyes a moment longer.

Chrissy was afraid she'd break. A trickle of sweat ran down her spine as she held his gaze.

His jaw tightened and he dropped his hand from her face. "As you wish." He turned away.

She exhaled the breath she'd been holding. "I'll bring you your clothes." As she walked from the room, tears stung her eyes and she brushed them away. It was for the best. It had been a sweet interlude, but she'd known from the beginning it couldn't last. Squaring her shoulders, Chrissy went to the bathroom to change.

"Can I at least take you out for breakfast?" Taylor asked, watching John slip on his shoes. "You can see a little bit of the city before you leave, and you'll have a really bizarre memory you can cherish and wonder if you hallucinated for the rest of your days."

He straightened, brushing his hair back from his forehead like she longed to. "Sure. I guess that'd be okay."

"Lila won't be home for over an hour. We have plenty of time."

Taylor took him to Starbucks for a king-sized muffin and a latte.

John glanced at the logo over the door before they went inside. "I've heard of Starbucks, a very popular chain at the turn of the century."

"Uh, yeah." Taylor led the way to the queue waiting for their morning fix. "What do you have instead?"

"Juice-Aholics. People don't drink coffee anymore. Juice blends are the current trend."

"You're shitting me. No coffee? How do you live?"

John laughed. "Healthier."

It was the first time she'd heard him laugh and she loved it. He had a deep, throaty chuckle that made her lips automatically turn up.

"Most coffee plantations were destroyed in earthquakes and mudslides or wiped out by a disease that attacked the plants. Believe me, you don't want to know about the escalating natural disasters over the next sixty years. Anyway, coffee's like gold. The average person can't buy it anymore."

She raised an eyebrow. "And you want to go back there? Libido suppressants and no coffee—what kind of world is that?" She moved up in line.

"Hey, at least there's no war," he countered.

"No war? As in none?"

"Border skirmishes here and there sometimes, but nothing like the world you're used to. It goes back to your friend's invention of the translator. You can't imagine how getting an accurate picture of what another person is trying to say can erase all the confusion that escalates to warfare."

The previous evening Taylor had been flip about Lila's genius status, but now it hit home that her friend really was amazing to have created something so important. "That's phenomenal! Good for Lila."

After they got their coffee and muffins, they located a table outdoors. A stiff breeze blew, but the sun shone, combating the cool temperature with its warm rays.

"So," Taylor said after she'd devoured the puffy top off her muffin. "You mentioned your mother. Is she the only family you have?"

"Yes. My father died when I was young and my mother remarried but divorced several years later. Both of my grandparents are dead now."

"I'm incapable of not being nosy. How did you end up as your mother's pawn?"

"It's not like that." He sipped his coffee then cursed as he burned his mouth.

"It sounds like she's counting on you to take care of her."

John frowned. "She's always had someone. First my dad, then Frank. She's used to having a certain standard of living."

"Hey, we'd all like to have money, but some of us have to earn it for ourselves. Sorry. I'm mouthy. Just tell me to shut up."

Without answering, he lifted his coffee mug and blew across the surface.

Taylor's eyes lowered as she imagined him blowing across her skin with those soft, puffy lips.

"What about your family?" he changed the subject. "Tell me your story."

"Big family. Little house. Lots of brothers and sisters always bickering. Me in the middle. My parents celebrated their forty-fifth wedding anniversary last year. So I'm one of those dinosaurs from a two-parent home. We're a very traditional family."

"Sounds nice."

"Try sharing a room with a sister who's a neat freak and see how nice it is. My sister, Ashley, ended up splitting our room in half with a line of masking tape down the middle." She laughed. "Even then we fought—name-calling, hair-pulling, clawing, rolling-across-the-floor fights. It was that way right up until Ash graduated and I finally had the room to myself. It was surprisingly quiet and lonely after that."

John smiled.

Taylor wanted to offer him more things to smile about because she'd discovered a small dimple in his right cheek. She told more family anecdotes and about scrapes she'd gotten herself into in high school and college. She talked to make him smile and laugh, and every time he did, it was like a sunburst.

"This coffee is really good," he said, during a break in her monologue. "I can see why people were addicted to it. I know my grandparents used to reminisce about coffee like it was nectar of the gods."

"Hey, none of your grandparents were named Hodgson, were they?" she asked. "It suddenly occurred to me we could actually be related somehow."

John laughed again. "No Hodgsons. You're not my great-gran."

"That's good. I don't want to be your granny." Taylor brushed her foot against his leg underneath the table and ran it lightly up his calf so he would have no doubt it wasn't an accident.

His eyes widened and he sucked in a breath with his next sip of coffee, setting him choking.

She grinned and removed her foot from his inseam. "Sorry. I'm just a poor, backward, turn-of-the-century girl and I'm *not* on a libido suppressant."

She teased him unmercifully, goading and amusing him and making him laugh. The permanent crease between his eyebrows all but disappeared. Taylor was pleased. In a very short time, she'd managed to open up this repressed man and bring him a little bit of joy. Her teachers had always scolded her for cutting up in class and distracting others, but it turned out the skill was useful.

Suddenly she remembered the agenda for the rest of the day. John was going home. She felt a stab of disappointment at the fleeting nature of their budding friendship. "We'd better get back. Lila's pissed enough at me already."

"Yes." John's smile disappeared. His face closed again and he resumed his habitual reserved expression.

Reaching her hand across the table, she placed it on his arm. "Are you sure you want to go back? You don't have to, you know. At least not right away."

He looked at her hand for a moment and touched it briefly with his own. "I'd really like to stay, but...I don't know if that's a good idea."

Taylor didn't ask why. She understood. If they started something, it would be hard to walk away from it. She removed her hand from his arm.

"Thanks for the coffee," he said quietly. "It was really good."

Somehow she felt he was thanking her for much more.

When they returned to the house, Lila was back and waiting for them. She pounced on Taylor like a cat on a hapless chipmunk, but only got as far as "Taylor!" before she was transfixed by the sight of John.

He walked into the living room, extending his hand and speaking as reverently as if addressing the Dalai Lama. "Ms. Janzen, it's such an honor. I can't believe I'm actually meeting you."

Lila's eyes widened in surprise as he grasped her hand and shook it.

"Seems you're somebody in the future," Taylor explained. "Your translator is a big deal."

"What?"

John nodded. "It's true. The basic design is still in use, but modified so it can be implanted." He indicated just behind his ear where there was an almost-invisible surgical scar.

"You're kidding." Lila's eyes went even wider. "You're wearing one now?"

"Yes. I had an implant when I took the job at Globalcon."

"But I wasn't going to tell anyone about this invention," she protested. "I decided last night to get rid of it along with the time machine."

Chrissy walked toward them from the living room. "You can't! John told us this translator made a major impact on the world—politics, business, everything. You have to present it to the scientific community. You can't simply bury this technology."

"It's too important," John agreed.

"Well, all right. I suppose the translator is useful." Lila frowned. "But the time machine definitely has to be destroyed as soon as I send you both home." She looked past John at Gareth who sat on the couch. The big man was stone faced and dour, and also a little ludicrous, dressed in his worn animal hides with his sword leaning against the end table beside him.

Taylor raised an eyebrow at Chrissy. She'd been positive her friend was going to plead for Gareth to stay, but if anything she seemed eager to be rid of him.

"We should get this over with." Chrissy's face was pale and a frown was etched between her eyebrows. "Send them back before something else goes wrong."

"Definitely." Lila led the way upstairs with the others trailing behind her.

Lila was the first into her room and walked straight to the time machine to gaze at the monitor. She couldn't suppress the frisson of excitement that ran up her spine at the idea of gazing into the future. But the picture on the monitor wasn't anything like the optimistic, peaceful portrait John had painted. Bombed buildings and running people in a haze of smoke were frozen on the screen.

John joined her by the monitor. "This isn't right." His voice rose in alarm. "This isn't where Taylor paused it."

Taylor squeezed in between them to take a look. "Um. No. That's definitely not the place I got John from."

"Oh Jesus, what did you do?"

"Nothing. I swear. See, the date is still the same, but the picture's different."

"Let me see." Chrissy pulled Taylor out of the way so she could look. "My God, it looks a war zone."

Lila felt a nudge against her other shoulder as Gareth crowded against her to get a look at the future. "What do the words on the wall say?"

Aloud, Chrissy read the messages of rebellion scrawled on the side of the building. "Let it play, Lila."

She set the picture in motion. The furtive runners dodged across the street just as a grenade or bomb exploded, showering them with rubble and bits of concrete. For a moment, the scene was obscured by smoke and debris.

"That's not my world," John whispered. "What the hell happened?"

Lila halted the motion again. "Something changed between last night and now. Something that affected the future."

There was a second of silence then everyone spoke at once, offering an opinion or comment.

"Hey," Taylor said, "I didn't have anything to do with this, I swear. But it's clear John can't go back to *that*. He'll have to stay here now."

"Perhaps a more powerful witch has taken control of your invention," Gareth suggested.

"I think it's the translator," Chrissy offered. "You decided not to share the technology with the world and it changed the course of events."

"But I changed my mind," Lila protested. "I said I *would*. I mean, I will, so nothing should have changed."

"Wait!" John's voice was urgent. "What's the date today?"

"September thirteenth." Taylor jostled Lila's arm as she tried to squeeze between Lila and Chrissy for another look.

"My God!" he exclaimed. "This is the day when the Janzen translator was first introduced at a meeting between Senator Howard Baines of Illinois and Chien Wu, a Chinese diplomat, prior to a Global Summit meeting. It made such an impact on trade relations that day the translator was quickly manufactured and distributed at the U.N. and at the Summit meeting. It enhanced communication between the countries so much—the world was never the same again."

"So, I'm supposed to present my invention to Senator Baines today before this meeting?" Lila asked. "That's impossible. How would someone like me get to speak to a senator, and how would I have known that's what I'm supposed to do if you hadn't told me? I never would have thought of it or known a private meeting was taking place."

"I don't know. I'm only telling you what I remember from history lessons."

Taylor chimed in excitedly. "Don't you see? It's fate. John was *meant* to come here to tell you this. I was *supposed* to bring him here from the future in order to make things work out right."

Gareth nodded and grunted an agreement. "The stars are set. We can only follow our destiny."

"Destiny, bullshit," Lila muttered. "It's not logical."

"Yes!" Chrissy spoke up. "Yes, it is. John is supposed to be here. He belongs here." Chrissy looked at Gareth with shining eyes as she spoke about John making it clear who she was really thinking about.

Lila sighed, wishing Zach was here to help her deal with this new crisis. She missed him already, although they'd only been apart a few hours. "All right. Where's this meeting and when?"

John frowned. "If I remember my history it was in a suite at the Belden Stratford Hotel. I don't know what time."

"How am I supposed to get to the senator?" she demanded.

"Don't worry," Taylor said. "This is working out exactly as it must. John delivered the message. Now all you have to do is follow through on it. Everything will fall into place since it's meant to be."

Somehow Lila doubted it would be that easy.

"If you won't let me bring my sword, at least let me bring my knife," Gareth said. "I can hold the guards off while the rest of you interrupt the council and talk to the lord."

"Thank you," Lila said. "But I think maybe it's best if you and Chrissy stay here."

Gareth scowled at her refusal of his help. But when Chrissy smiled at him, his frown evaporated. "Very well."

Lila looked back and forth between them. Separating them and sending Gareth back to the past might be difficult. However, she could only deal with one problem at a time, so she put the thought out of her mind.

Twenty minutes later, John, Lila and Taylor left Zach's car in a nearby parking garage and walked to the Belden Stratford. They entered the opulent old hotel and scanned the few guests present in the lobby.

"I don't even know what our senator looks like," Taylor admitted.

"He looks like that." Lila nodded at a man with salt-and-pepper hair and a smartly tailored, charcoal gray suit, who strode purposefully across the lobby. An aide speaking into a headphone and another carrying a briefcase flanked him.

"Wow. That was easy," Taylor whispered. "See, I told you it was all meant to be."

"No bodyguards?" John asked. "Your generation is known for its paranoia about terrorism. I would have thought all government officials would be heavily guarded."

"Come on. Quick, before he gets in the elevator." Lila crossed the plush carpet in pursuit of Baines.

John grabbed her arm. "Wait. Let us distract the aides while you get the senator's attention."

Her heart raced. She hadn't been this frightened since her clarinet solo in middle school band at the big spring concert. She remembered how badly that had turned out, the notes she knew like her own name skittering out of reach and her performance going from horrible to excruciating. *Can't choke. No time to choke,* she reprimanded herself as Taylor and John approached the rapidly moving senator and his aides.

She moved around the perimeter of the room, planning to tackle Baines at an oblique angle while his aides were occupied with Taylor's chatter. Lila couldn't hear what Taylor said as she and John hailed the senator, but recognized the rapid, sing-song lilt of her voice from across the lobby.

The two aides moved to intercept Taylor and John as they walked toward Baines. The senator halted in his progress toward the elevator. Lila caught a flash of annoyance cross his face before he manufactured a smile for his constituents' benefit. Baines spoke briefly to his aides and they parted like the Red Sea, allowing him to shake hands with Taylor and John.

Lila scurried toward the senator. She was now between him and the elevator. The backs of all three tailored jackets were to her as she reached him. "Excuse me, sir."

None of the men responded.

Lila clutched the two translators in her hands and spoke up more loudly. "Excuse me, Senator Baines."

He turned at the sound of his name and looked at Lila curiously. "Yes?"

"I have something very important to tell you." Her pulse pounded in her ears and she felt like she might pass out from lack of oxygen. She extended the devices toward Baines. "There's something you should—"

The headphone aide quickly intercepted her, stepping between Lila and the senator and grabbing at her arm. The briefcase aide was right behind him, clutching her shoulder and pushing her back, away from Baines. Meanwhile, two hotel security guards in navy blazers entered the action, appearing from nowhere to flank Senator Baines.

"No. It's not a weapon." Lila opened her hand to show the device. "It's a translator. I thought the senator might be able to use it during his talk with—"

"I'm sorry, miss, you'll have to make an appointment through the office to meet with Senator Baines. I can give you a phone number to call." As Headphone Aide spoke, he nodded at the hotel security guards.

Like a choreographed dance, the partners changed. The security guards moved toward Lila and the aides flocked back to Baines.

Taylor pressed forward. "Excuse me. This lady is one of your constituents. Are you going to let her be strong-armed like this?"

"The senator is on his way to an important meeting," Briefcase Aide said smoothly, conducting Baines toward the elevator.

"Sir." John followed them. "You don't understand. National security is at stake."

One of the security guards intercepted John, taking him by the elbow, and another guard covered Taylor.

The elevator doors closed behind the senator and his aides. Lila, Taylor and John were politely but firmly escorted from the Belden Stratford Hotel.

Outside, Taylor let loose a stream of profanity. "We're Americans, dammit. Can't we even talk to our elected officials?"

"There has to be a way back in the building. Maybe a fire escape." John looked speculatively up the height of the hotel.

"I suppose we should be glad we weren't arrested," Lila said. "But what are we going to do now?"

For a moment they stared gloomily at the building from which they'd been ejected. Then suddenly, John's face lit up. "The time machine! We have all the time in the world. We'll wait at the top for the elevator to arrive. Gareth and I will restrain those aides and you can talk to the senator."

"Will he even listen to me?"

"Of course. He has to," Taylor said confidently. "Remember, all of this is supposed to happen."

Lila really wished she'd quit saying that.

The moment the others left the house, Gareth turned to Chrissy with a questioning look. He could tell from her earlier smile her attitude had changed.

She took his hand. "I'm sorry I've been so cold to you today. I wanted you to return home, because I thought it was best for your health and, maybe because I was afraid to commit. But what Taylor said about this being inevitable struck me. I'm still nervous. It's all so sudden and unexpected." She gripped his hand tighter and looked at him with her wide, green eyes. "But I can't deny the connection between us. I can't deny what I feel when I'm with you."

Chrissy rested one of her hands lightly on his chest and he felt his heart rising to meet it. "What you and Taylor believe about destiny," she continued, "I've never really taken that view of life. But every moment since I first saw you has felt...familiar somehow, like it was supposed to be this way. I think we were brought together for a reason and I don't want to lose you." She swallowed hard and blinked the brightness from her eyes.

Gareth exhaled. He felt like he'd been holding his breath for the past three days. He opened his arms and Chrissy stepped into his embrace. Holding her tight and breathing in the sweet scent of her hair, he felt like he'd reached home.

Even though there was no need to rush, Lila drove too fast on the way home. The sense of urgency carried the three of them from the car, into the house and upstairs to the time machine.

"Unbelievable! We're in the middle of a crisis and they're at it again," Taylor exclaimed as they reached the second floor landing and heard sexual groans coming from Chrissy's room. "You guys go on ahead. I'll get them."

As Lila and John continued to the third floor, Taylor pounded on Chrissy's door, yelling at her to "lay off the nookie and get dressed".

The monitor was exactly as they'd left it, frozen on another image of warfare. Lila sighed. She'd hoped somehow, magically, things would have changed just by her meeting the senator. Sitting in the control chair, she set the parameters for the current date, year and location.

As the day played out, Lila focused on herself, watching with fascination as she went through her day—kissing Zach goodbye, driving home and learning about the future all in fast forward mode. It was eerie and disorienting.

She slowed the scene down as it neared the past hour and the events at the hotel.

Taylor, with Chrissy and Gareth still buttoning and zipping themselves into clothes, joined Lila and John at the monitor. "Oh my God, there we are. It's so weird."

They watched as the hotel guards hustled the trio out of the lobby then Lila changed focus, following the senator and his aides into the elevator.

"See what floor he picks." Chrissy tapped the glass screen urgently.

Lila zeroed in on a finger pressing the button for the top floor. Then she changed location to the empty hallway by the executive suite on the top floor of the hotel. In another moment the elevator would open and Senator Baines would arrive.

Lila froze time. She wondered how long your system could be flooded with adrenaline before your heart simply exploded from it. She felt as jittery as if she'd drunk a twenty-gallon pot of coffee. Now that the actual moment for being hurtled through time had arrived, she found she was terrified of it—not to mention confronting the senator again on the other end.

"Okay, this is it," Taylor said. "Who's going and who's staying to operate the machine? Lila, are you positive this thing works right?"

"Gareth and I will go with her," John said. "Hopefully we can keep these guys in the elevator, leaving Baines alone in the hall with Lila."

"I'll take my—"

"No, Gareth. No knives or swords," Chrissy interrupted. "And try not to punch these guys either, just restrain them."

Gareth grimaced.

"All right," Lila blew out a shaky breath. "Let's do this."

"That was a little alarming," Howard Baines said to his secretary, James Finch.

"You should have a bodyguard, sir," Finch replied, glancing at his Palm Pilot and reviewing notes for the meeting. "If that woman had a gun... Carl and I aren't equipped to deal with situations like that."

"He's right, sir," Carl Nesmith agreed. It didn't matter who was speaking or how many times he switched sides, he always agreed.

"Well, maybe I'll consider it." Baines mentally reviewed his limited knowledge of Chinese. "Hello" and "Honored to meet you" were about the extent of it. "Do you know who our translator is?"

Finch consulted his Pilot. "Yiang Chen, Chinese born, Stanford educated. He's lived in the U.S. for ten years. He's good, sir."

"Excellent. This is a delicate situation. I don't want any misunderstandings to—"

The elevator door slid open and the senator started in surprise. Standing in the hall facing him was the frantic African American woman from the lobby, the blond man he'd shaken hands with and a big, bearded man, who looked like a club bouncer.

Finch was a quick thinker. After one glance at the trio, he lunged for the button to close the elevator door.

"Wait, sir, no, if you'll just listen," the woman blurted.

At the same moment, the bouncer pushed into the elevator and seized Finch's hand in a bone-crushing grip. A little slower but right on his heels, the blond man went for Nesmith.

The big man shoved Baines through the open door into the hallway. The elevator doors closed behind him, leaving him alone with the strange woman.

"I'm so sorry about this," she said in a rush. "If you'll just listen to me with an open mind, I'll make this brief so you can get on with your meeting."

"How do you know about the meeting?" Baines stared at the woman, considering pushing her down and running for the door of the suite. But his curiosity and her earnest expression made him hesitate. He wanted to hear her story.

"My name is Lila Janzen. I'm a scientist. I invented a translating device which I think you'll find very useful. It works based on thought patterns instead of actual language which makes the translation much more precise."

"How did you get up here so quickly?" Baines interrupted.

"It doesn't matter, and you wouldn't believe me if I told you, sir. The important thing is that you *have* to use this device at this particular meeting. Important things hinge on this moment in time. Please don't ask me what or how I know."

He was dumbfounded. The situation was surreal. "You're asking me to take a lot on faith," he said, stalling for time while he figured out what to do.

"I know that, sir. I know this whole thing seems crazy. You don't know me at all, but I'm asking you to trust me. Please!"

The senator from Illinois gazed into Lila Janzen's serious, dark eyes and saw she was telling the truth. At least, she believed she was. "Let me see this device."

She extended her hand, offering him two small objects that looked like hearing aids.

"How can I test these before the meeting? You don't expect me to simply take your word."

"Of course not. Um... Do you speak French?"

"Only a few phrases."

"Then, please sir, put the translator on and listen."

Reluctantly, Baines put the device in his ear.

The woman began speaking to him. "I took French all four years of high school. I can't remember it well, but hope I am expressing myself clearly. Do you understand me?"

It was amazing. He could simultaneously hear the actual French words coming out of her mouth and understand their meaning in his head. "Y-yes," he stammered. "I understand." He took the invention from his ear and examined it closely. "Say something else," he asked.

Lila spoke a few more phrases, which meant absolutely nothing to him although he thought he caught the word for "hat". Baines put the device back in his ear in time to catch her next words. "...dog ate my new shoes. I would like a crepe, please. Can you tell me the way to the Eiffel Tower?"

"Unbelievable! It works." He looked sharply at Lila. "But how did you know about this meeting? And how—"

"Please, sir, no more questions. It would sound so farfetched, I couldn't begin to explain it to you, and you're going to be late for your meeting if we keep talking. Just use these today. Contact me afterward and we'll talk." She thrust a square of paper with her name and a scrawled phone number into Baines' hand. "And please don't have me or my friends arrested. We didn't mean any harm and had to get your attention."

Just then the elevator doors slid open again to show the four men inside.

"Finished?" the blond man asked. He still had Nesmith pinned to the wall with an arm across the man's throat.

"Are we?" Lila looked at Baines with a raised eyebrow.

He examined the earpiece once more, turning it over and over in his hand then made a gut decision. "Yes. I think this device is astounding and I'll use it at the meeting today." He glanced at Finch, who was red-faced and sweating, his arm drawn up behind his back by the big, dark-haired man. "Tell your friends to let my aides go and we'll pretend this didn't happen."

The blond man instantly stepped away from Nesmith. The bouncer grumbled something unintelligible then released Finch with a shove.

Lila shook Baines' hand. "Thank you so much, sir. You don't know how important this was."

He didn't ask for more explanation she wouldn't give. But somewhere deep inside he felt a vague sense of impending doom diverted. Perhaps this meeting with Chien Wu was even more critical than he'd thought. "Thank you, Ms. Janzen. I'll be in touch."

Baines beckoned his disgruntled aides forward and they headed toward the ambassador suite. Glancing back, he caught a last glimpse of Lila Janzen as the elevator door closed. He thought he heard her say, "Beam me up, Scotty," then suddenly the elevator was empty before the doors closed completely.

The time travel machine suddenly overflowed with bodies. Chrissy and Taylor had been sharing the driver's seat as they sent Lila and the men back through time then called them home. Five bodies now crowded in the booth instead of two.

Taylor pushed the mountain of Gareth out of her face. "Jesus, Lila, could you have made this booth any smaller?"

In moments they'd sorted themselves out, spilling from the cubicle like clowns from a circus car.

"Did it work?" Lila elbowed John aside and went to the control panel, to change the picture from the empty elevator to a city street sixty years in the future.

Taylor peered over her shoulder. The street scene was normal. It looked like downtown on any given Sunday, except the clothing and some of the architecture was different, and the ads above the storefronts moved in holographic splendor. She felt a surge of relief and a stab of disappointment. There was nothing to keep John from returning home now. She glanced at the handsome blond man watching the monitor. "Everything look normal?" Lila asked.

"Yeah." He nodded. "Just the same as always." He looked at Taylor then back to the screen.

"Fantastic! I'll find the exact moment where you belong and send you home before something else happens." Lila bent to the control panel.

John watched his life go by in fast motion as Lila located him then searched for the moment from which he'd been seized. This was it—the sum of his days? It was almost unbearable to see himself rushing through the minutes and hours of his life, doing what he was told, learning what society dictated he learn, working at a job that meant nothing to him and sleeping alone at night.

When Lila reached the precise moment from which he'd been plucked and the moving images froze, he felt queasy. One thought filled his mind and suddenly, words to match the thought spilled out of his mouth. "No! I can't go back."

"What?" Lila looked at him sharply.

"I don't want to go back." He stepped out of the booth as if she might hit a switch and force him to go. "Not yet." *Maybe not ever.*

"But—"

"Lila, you heard him. He doesn't want to go. You can't make him," Taylor crowed triumphantly.

John watched her as he'd been doing off and on all day. With all the drama, he wouldn't have expected to have time to dwell on Taylor's face, her hair, her hips or her breasts. But even in the midst of the crisis every time his arm brushed hers it felt electrified. He'd lost his train of thought when he glanced at her and caught her blue eyes looking back at him. There was no doubt the Dorancian had worn off. His cock was in a permanent state of semi-arousal, his senses heightened and everything smelled stronger, sounded clearer, looked brighter than before.

Arms folded, Taylor moved between John and the time machine. "We're not Nazis here. We can't make people do what they don't want to do? Right, Chrissy?"

Chrissy drew a deep breath and clutched Gareth's hand. "She's right, Lila. Gareth's not going back, either. He's staying here with me. I don't care if it screws up history. Hell, he's been gone from his time for three days now and nothing seems any different."

"I won't go," he added firmly.

Lila rose from her seat. "This is serious. We can't mess with the order of things."

"This *is* the order of things." Chrissy said. "Look around. Everyone's happy. Everything's good. These guys want to stay. Let it go."

"How would you feel if someone sent Zach away?" Taylor asked.

"I..." Lila stared at the machine then at each of the mutinous people surrounding her. She shook her head. "Fine. I give up. This machine goes down tomorrow and anyone who isn't back in his proper time by then is stuck here forever." She glared at John. "Are you ready for that? Being stuck in the olden-days with all our primitive ways forever?"

Taylor turned toward John and raised an eyebrow over one twinkling, blue eye.

A grin spread across his face. "Yeah. Forever sounds really good to me."

Chapter Eleven

"Look at them all. Disgusting!" Several weeks later, Lila leaned against the kitchen doorway, looking into the living room where the three men watched auto racing on TV. The guys couldn't have looked more different—or more the same.

Tall, skinny Zach sat on the living room floor with his long legs sprawled in front of him, leaning back against the couch. He glanced over his shoulder at Gareth as he explained the differences in race engines versus regular car engines. His shaggy, dirty-blond head bobbed as he talked animatedly, using a lot of hand gestures to illustrate his words.

Gareth solemnly nodded his understanding. His dark eyes never lifted from the endless circle of cars whining past on the TV screen. He was huge and his neck and limbs so thick and muscled he made gangly Zach look scrawny by comparison.

Then there was John lounging in the armchair, one leg hooked comfortably over the arm. His fine-featured beauty gave him the appearance of an ethereal angel, but he was clearly all man as he refused to surrender the remote control. It was gripped in his hand and at every commercial break, he'd switch from the race to the NBA game until Zach complained and made him turn it back again.

Gareth watched either sport with the same rapt attention he gave daytime soaps, infomercials, *CSI* episodes and *Mythbusters* reruns.

"They're watching TV and we're in the kitchen," Chrissy complained, coming up behind Lila. "Who wrote this script? I feel like I'm in my grandma's house."

"Don't worry," Taylor said from over near the stove where she was stirring sauce. "The boys'll get all the clean-up afterward, guaranteed."

"Oh, you'd better believe it," Lila said.

"You have to admit it's sweet to see them bonding." Chrissy cast an affectionate eye on Gareth.

Sitting around the dinner table a half-hour later, the six raised their glasses in a toast.

"To Lila," John said, "without whom half of us wouldn't be here today. I feel like you not only changed my life, but gave it back to me. I would've kept on walking through my days half-asleep and lived the rest of my life like that." He smiled at Taylor. "I'm glad I didn't have to."

"Here, here," Zach, Chrissy and Taylor chimed in, while Gareth muttered something unintelligible.

"And here's to the men," Taylor said, "for being men and giving us plenty of big O's."

The women laughed and drank to it.

Gareth reclined on Chrissy's bed, totally nude, arms folded behind his head. She felt him watching her as she went through her nightly routine, combing her hair and applying almond-scented lotion to her legs and arms. She adjusted the bodice on the new, silky negligee she'd bought and put on her earpiece so she could understand him whether he spoke in his own language or in broken English.

Behind her on the bed, he growled. "Come, woman. Hurry."

The hair rose on her nape the way it always did when he used his growly, alpha tone. She'd never admit it to Taylor or Lila, but she liked Gareth's aggressive, commanding ways in the bedroom. She also loved the way he spoke in little phrases and hoped he'd never completely lose his rough accent.

"Coming." Chrissy turned from the bureau and walked across the room, her nightgown whispering around her legs and brushing her skin seductively. She gazed at the gorgeous sight of her man, so dark and wild against the purity of the white cotton sheets. His hair curled around the harsh bones of his face, softening it. His eyes glowed as they scanned her body from head to toe. The lines of his muscles were sharply defined from his big biceps to his hard chest, flat stomach and thick, hairy legs. His erection jutted out from a dark tangle of hair, vibrating with energy, beckoning her to touch it.

She sat on the bed beside him and ran her hand up his leg from calf to muscled thigh. Then, with a smile, she stroked her hand in between his thighs until she reached the heavy sac nestled there.

He smiled as he watched her fondle his balls and sucked in a breath through his teeth when she slid her hand up his veined shaft all the way to the swollen head of his cock.

Chrissy brushed her thumb over the moist slit on the smooth, round head, already protruding from his foreskin. She glided her hand up and down his length several times until he groaned. Slowly she bent over, watching his avid eyes as she wrapped her lips around the head of his cock and drew him in her mouth. She relished the salty taste of his flesh and the musky flavor of pre-come.

"Mmm," Gareth groaned, resting his big, heavy hand on the crown of her head. "Iss gud."

Chrissy smiled and redoubled her efforts, stroking and sucking Gareth's thick cock until he was groaning steadily. She released him and crawled up his body to straddle his hips. Looking down into his eyes was like looking into two deep, dark wells.

He stroked the side of her face then cupped her nape and drew her down for a deep, searching kiss. His hot, wet tongue swept over hers, sending shafts of desire lancing through her body straight to her pussy. Her inner muscles clenched and released wetly. A yawning, yearning sensation swelled between her legs, begging to be filled.

Moaning into his mouth, she shifted her negligee-clad body on top of him and ground her crotch against his erection, pleasing them both. She kissed him deep and hungry then light and sweet, ending with a peck on his lips. She smiled as she gazed down on him. "I'm so glad you stayed."

He smiled back with smug arrogance and spoke in his own tongue. "Of course you are. Remember, I always know best, Chrissy."

"Hmph," she snorted, tugging lightly on the fringe of beard sculpting his jaw. She considered asking him to shave it so she could see what his chin looked like underneath, but, for now, just knowing he would do it if she asked him to was enough. As much as he liked to pretend to dominate her, they both knew who was really in control. He'd do anything to please her.

Gareth laughed and his eyes crinkled delightfully at the corners.

Chrissy couldn't resist and began kissing him again.

After a few moments of increasingly hungry kisses, he flipped her on her back and lay over her, supporting his weight on bulging biceps. It was his turn to look down into her eyes and to rub his hardness back and forth over her aching crotch. Her clit twitched, needing even more stimulation.

Gareth licked and kissed his way from her mouth to her throat then down the flat plane of her chest to the small mounds of her breasts. Through the sheer fabric of her peignoir he sucked one hard nipple into his mouth.

She moaned at the sensation of his hot mouth on her tit. Her back arched as she offered her chest up to him, moaning quietly.

Gareth chuckled around his mouthful of wet material and flesh. He cupped her other breast in his right hand, easily encompassing the small breast in his huge fist. He squeezed lightly then toyed with the pebbled aureola and hard nipple.

Chrissy squirmed beneath him as he tweaked and twisted the bud, sending mingled messages of pleasure and pain arching through her nervous system. "Ah," she sighed.

He growled in pleasure at the soft sound. Pulling his mouth from her breast, he suddenly grabbed the delicate fabric of the nightgown and ripped it open across her chest. It shredded easily, exposing her wet, naked tits to the cool air.

She gasped and her half-lidded eyes flew open wide. "I'm going to quit buying new lingerie if you keep ruining it! Barbarian!"

Gareth laughed and descended on her breasts once more like a hawk diving on two soft, vulnerable doves.

Zach couldn't get enough of Lila's tits. He loved to fondle, lick, bite and suck them until she practically came from the stimulation of his mouth on her breasts.

Lila twisted and cried out as he squeezed her breasts and pulled on her nipples, but eventually she'd had enough and urged him lower. "Go down on me, baby."

Obligingly he relinquished her mammaries and kissed his way down her twitching stomach toward her belly button. He swirled his tongue inside it, toying with the sapphire navel stud, then continued on his way toward her pelvis.

Her stomach leaped inside as well as out, muscles twitching rhythmically as Zach neared his target. She sucked in her breath and waited for him to lick her clit.

He settled his lanky body between her legs, pushing her thighs apart and planting his hands firmly on either side of her vagina. Then Zach began to tease her unmercifully, kissing slowly up the insides of her thighs, lapping between her plump folds, delving into her slippery channel, but refusing to satisfy her by giving even one tiny nibble on her erect bud. His soft hair brushed against her inner thigh as he bent his head even lower, licking back toward her anus. His tongue tickled her past endurance.

She writhed and moaned beneath his restraining hands. "Come on, you bastard. You're killing me," she whined. "Do me!"

"I don't know what you're talking about." He lifted his head and gazed at her with those guileless, wide, pale green eyes. "You know, I'm not the he-man type so I couldn't possibly be any good at...this." He flicked the tip of his finger lightly over her clit.

Lila gasped and bucked.

Zach grinned and descended on her tiny nub with the ferocity and finesse of a cat toying with a mouse. He nibbled and worried it then gently licked and soothed it. Then he stopped playing and slipped into the rhythm he knew she liked.

She felt a swelling tsunami coursing through her body as he lapped her clit. Squeezing her eyes tightly shut, she rode the wave like a surfer, the sensations rising, rising, rising and cresting then crashing on the shore of her consciousness. "Oh, God!" Her hips and lower back arched up high then landed on the bed with a soft thump.

"Mmm, nice," Zach whispered.

When Lila had recovered her breath and her senses, she opened her eyes to look at him, smiling at her from between her legs.

He kissed her belly then crawled up on top of her and kissed her mouth.

She could taste her essence on his tongue and it was earthy and rich. "My turn to play." She winked and flipped him on his back, pinning him to the bed.

Her heavy breasts brushed against his chest then she sat straight and tall on top of Zach, straddling his hips. Pressing her hands against his chest, she teased his straining cock with her wet pussy, letting him rest just inside her entrance but refusing to slide down on him. She grinned at Zach's dilated, desperate eyes. "You want it? Tell me how much."

"Much," he gritted through clenched teeth. "Very, very much."

She eased herself on top of his rigid erection, sheathing the head then another inch before pulling off him.

Zach groaned and grasped her hips, trying to seat her on himself, but she resisted.

"Nu-uh. Not yet." Again and again she let him inside her, a little bit, then a little bit more, but always pulled back before his cock was completely enveloped.

"Cold hearted, bitch," he gasped.

Lila laughed and rolled completely off him, got a foil packet from her nightstand, ripped it open and rolled a purple condom down his shaft.

He eyed it with a frown. "Purple? God, I hate the twenty-first century. I miss the old days of flesh on flesh."

"Now," Lila leaned down and kissed his chest. "You ready to try something new?"

"Will it hurt?"

"Not if we do it right."

"Does it end up with me coming?"

"Probably."

"Then I'm in."

She straddled Zach's hips again only this time positioned herself backwards, easing her pussy down on his shaft until he was deep inside her. She glanced over her shoulder to see his avidly staring at her backside.

"Whoa, that looks so hot," he muttered, running his hand down her spine all the way to the crack in her ass.

It was an odd angle of penetration. Lila braced her hands on his thighs and moved carefully as she rose and fell on him.

"Oh, yeah," he whispered, his hands stroking her ass, parting her cheeks so he could watch himself glide in and out. He wet his finger with her juices and moved it lightly around her anus before dipping inside the tight hole.

Lila gasped at the sensation and rode him a little harder. She reached between her splayed legs and fondled his balls, as she watched his glistening purple cock glide in and out of her depths. She felt his fingers pushing into her ass and stretching the tight ring of muscle. The sensation aroused her and she slowly, steadily increased her speed.

Zach thrust up hard inside her, groaning deeply.

John groaned deep in his throat as he thrust into Taylor faster and faster. She was pinned against the kitchen door, her legs wrapped around his hips. His hands cupped her ass, lifting her as pressed her against the door.

She gripped his shoulders and bore down on his cock, thrilled by his enthusiasm, riding him hard. Her breasts jiggled as she pistoned up and down.

He spun them away from the door and carried her to the kitchen table. Sweeping the detritus of their late night snack onto the floor, he laid her across it then climbed on top of her.

Grabbing his head, she pulled him down for a soul-sucking kiss while they fucked. He thrust into her fast and wild, desperate as an animal. Aroused by his frantic need, Taylor's orgasm rose quickly inside her. The coiling energy in her core grew stronger and tighter until it burst into an explosion of light and power that flooded her being. Taylor cried out and held onto John's biceps as she arched up from the table.

"Oh, God. Oh, Christ," he moaned as she clenched around him.

She grabbed his ass and dug her nails in, pulling him into her even harder.

John thrust only a few more times before releasing with an ecstatic cry.

Taylor opened her eyes to see his face twist in an agonized expression of bliss. She loved watching men come. Their feelings were so exposed, their guarded, macho exteriors shredded to expose real, raw emotions underneath. She sighed happily.

His blue eyes flickered open and he gazed down at her. He exhaled a long, slow breath. "Whew..."

"I know." She grinned smugly.

The kitchen around them was a shambles. It was surprising no one had come downstairs to check out the noise. She breathed John's scent in deeply and hugged his sweaty body against her.

He collapsed on top of her, pinning her to the table, and nuzzling her neck with his soft lips. "That was absolutely amazing."

"Uh-huh," she murmured contentedly.

His breath panted raggedly for a moment, then he said, "Can we do it again?"

"Abso-fucking-lutely."

Lila flopped on Zach's chest. His arms slipped around her and held her close. She kissed his overheated flesh and listened to his heartbeat.

He stroked his hand up her back and brought it to rest on her shoulder, playing with a lock of her hair. "That was amazing. Thanks."

"Thank *you*." She kissed his chest.

"I really like you a lot, Lila." He smiled and mimicked her first profession of caring. "I mean, I *like* you like you... Like a girlfriend."

She smiled and tweaked his nipple. "I really like you, too. A whole lot."

"Good. Does this mean we're 'going steady'? Should I dig up my old class ring?"

She linked her dark brown fingers with his long white ones. "Baby, you can give me any kind of ring you want. I won't turn it down."

Gareth wrapped an arm around Chrissy and pulled her back tight against his front. His body was like a hot engine, warming her backside, his arm a heavy band holding her close. He brushed her hair aside and kissed her right behind the ear then whispered in it, "*Ni amberia,* Chrissy."

She smiled and held onto his warm, naked arm. "I love you, too."

Three sets of lovers lay tangled in sleep in the early hours before dawn. Three women curled against the heat of their lover's bodies. All different, all the same. As it ever was and always would be, men and women were entwined.

About the Author

To learn more about Bonnie Dee, please visit http://bonniedee.com. Send an email to Bonnie Dee at bondav40@yahoo.com or join her Yahoo! http://groups.yahoo.com/group/bonniedee

Every good girl longs for a chance to be a little naughty.

Haley's Cabin
© *2007 Anne Rainey*

Raw from an ugly divorce and wrung out from her demanding job, Haley Thorne needs a break. When Haley's doctor urges her to take a vacation, she heads to her secret cabin in the woods.

The very first night, Haley dreams of an erotic threesome that leaves her panting and aroused. When sexy police detective Jeremy Pickett shows up at her door, she's shocked: He looks like the man in her midnight fantasy! Levelheaded Haley unleashes her inner seductress and has a little fun—handcuffs and all!

Available now in ebook from Samhain Publishing.

Enjoy the following excerpt...

Haley must still have been dreaming, because things this exciting just didn't happen to her. Frankly, she'd never met a man like Jay, or Jeremy, rather. He was so straightforward. He saw what he wanted and threw caution to the wind. After being married to Eric, a man who put on a façade to get what he wanted, it was a refreshing change to meet a guy who felt no need to pretend.

Right at that moment Haley was a few scant inches away from Jay's impressive chest. God, he looked delicious. She had visions of coasting her tongue over and around each of his nipples, down his torso, then unbuttoning his jean shorts. She'd watch them fall to the floor. Then she'd get to see his erection. Haley wanted her mouth on his cock. She ached to taste him. Honesty forced her to admit she wanted what he'd done to her in her dreams. This was a vacation, after all. A moment out of time. Haley yearned to take some memories back with her on Monday, when her fantasy ended and real life intruded. Something that would last her a lifetime.

After spending an erotic weekend with Jay/Jeremy Pickett, Haley had a sneaky feeling other men were going to seem pale in comparison.

"Can you take off your shorts for me, Jay?" Haley asked, feeling bolder now her mind was made up to take what she could from their encounter.

Jay smiled and in a hoarse whisper replied, "I already took off my top. It's your turn."

Okay, so he was going to play hard to get. No problem.

"It's not really fair, though, because this dress is all I'm wearing." *Take that,* she thought haughtily.

Jay's gaze went south, bypassing her chest and going straight to the notch between her legs. She could have sworn she felt heat there, just from the intensity of his stare.

His silvery eyes changed to liquid mercury. His words nearly melted her in the chair. "My cock is going to feel so damn good inside you, Haley. So good you'll forget all about your erotic dream. You'll beg me, baby. That's a promise."

He stood to his full, impressive height and took off his shorts right there in front of her. Oh my, he was every bit as big as he'd been in her dream. He was full and hard and so ready for her that her mouth watered from the sight. All she'd need do was lean forward and he'd be inside her wet mouth.

With his feet braced apart, a hard, predatory look on his face, he demanded, "The dress, Haley, off with it."

He was no longer the friendly, flirtatious man she'd eaten dinner with. Now Jay was an aggressive and dominant male. The raw masculinity of him turned her on more than anything ever had. If she hadn't felt so confident about herself, the sheer size of him might've intimidated her. Haley *was* confident, however. She'd gained her confidence the hard way. And she knew, no matter how intimidating he seemed, he'd never hurt her.

Without standing, Haley slipped her fingers beneath the hem of her dress and inched it upward. By small degrees she bared her thighs. As she reached her bottom, she had to lift slightly to get the dress higher. Soon, it was around her middle. She didn't get any farther. Jay's hand was suddenly there, cupping her exposed mound. His nostrils flared and his jaw twitched, as if he wanted to do much more than touch. She liked the thought. Haley wasn't the type to drive men mindless and it was empowering to realize she had that effect on Jay.

She wiggled, and he moved his hand away, seemingly reluctantly, and she took the dress off the rest of the way. Haley sat in the hard wooden kitchen chair, totally nude, while she let him look his fill. She only hoped he liked what he saw or she would absolutely die of mortification.

As if reading her thoughts, Jay groaned. "You look so sweet sitting there. So bashful with your legs pressed tight together." He snared her gaze with his own. "I can't wait to spread you open, to see that lovely cunt dripping from the first orgasm I give you, baby."

She couldn't think. Couldn't even speak. Jay had taken the heavy weight of his cock in his hand and began rubbing himself as he spoke to her. The sight of him mesmerized Haley. His words penetrated, and she managed to ask, "*First* orgasm?"

A slow grin spread across his face as he crouched in front of her. He leaned forward and took her nipple into his mouth, softly suckling on her.

"Oh, God."

Jay laved at her, loving in his assault. Haley could have come right there, without him so much as touching her clit.

Abruptly, he stood, staring down at her now glistening breast. "I'm really going to enjoy playing with your pretty tits." He stopped touching himself and took her hand, pulling her out of the cold chair and leading her to the backdoor. When he opened it, a rush of brisk night air came in and she was reminded of the dream once again. It was chilly then, too, when she'd let him and Marissa into her house.

Together, they stepped out onto a stone walkway leading to a secluded spot which hid the Jacuzzi. Thick shrubs and colorful flowers formed a wall around it. They were in their own private paradise.

As he took her to the side of the hot tub, Haley noticed he'd set out candles. All shapes and sizes glowed everywhere—on the ground, the little outdoor table next to the tub and along one edge of the walk. The sweet smell of vanilla permeated the air. She wanted to comment on the romance of it all, but before she could, Jay leaned down and whispered another erotic promise into her ear.

"I'll make you come so many times you'll wish to be my sex slave." He licked the spot beneath her ear, and her body shook and her mind went blank. "I'm going to turn you into a little wanton." He moved farther down her neck, tasting her, nibbling on her overheated skin. "My own private submissive," Jay promised, then he lifted away from her and ordered, "Get into the water now."

She obeyed. There was really never any other choice. Every fiber of her being was tuned in and turned on, and she longed to submit to him. Just as he promised, she already ached to be his dutiful slave.

GREAT
cheap
fUN

Discover eBooks!

THE FASTEST WAY TO GET THE HOTTEST NAMES

Get your favorite authors on your favorite reader, long before they're
out in print! Ebooks from Samhain go wherever you go, and work with
whatever you carry—Palm, PDF, Mobi, and more.

samhain
publishing Ltd

WWW.SAMHAINPUBLISHING.COM